Bram Stoker

Dracula
吸血殭屍

Adaptation and activities
by Janet Borsbey and Ruth Swan
Illustrated by Valerio Vidali

The Commercial Press

Contents 目錄

故事錄音開始和結束的標記
start ▶ **stop** ◼

Bram Stoker started writing his notes for *Dracula* around 1890. The story takes place around then. He tells the story using diary entries and letters from the main characters.

Count Dracula

A mysterious man
from Transylvania.

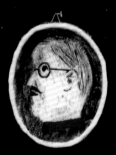

Dr John Seward

A young doctor.
He works in a psychiatric hospital.
He is in love
with Lucy Westenra.

R. M. Renfield

One of Dr Seward's patients.

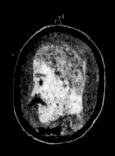

Jonathan Harker

A young lawyer.
He is the first person
we meet in the story.
He is engaged to Mina.

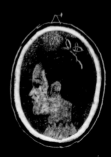

Mina

She is engaged
to Jonathan Harker.
She is intelligent and kind.

Lucy Westenra

Mina's best friend.
She loves
Arthur Holmwood.

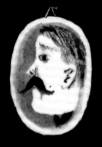

Quincey P. Morris

A friend of Dr Seward
and Arthur Holmwood.
is an American, from Texas.
He is also in love
with Lucy Westenra.

Arthur Holmwood

A friend of Dr Seward.
He wants to marry
Lucy Westenra.

Professor Van Helsing

Older than the other
characters. He was
Dr Seward's professor.
He is from Holland. He helps
everyone in the story.

Grammar

1 **Irregular Verbs Wordsearch. Find the past tense of the verbs in the wordsearch and complete the sentences.**

1 Count Dracula __*took*__ (take) me to his castle.

2 I _____ (leave) Munich at 8.35 on 1st May.

3 The driver's hat _____ (hide) his face.

4 I _____ (see) the castle in the distance.

5 I _____ (wake) up late and went downstairs.

6 Count Dracula _____ (throw) a bag on the floor.

7 I _____ (write) two letters, yesterday.

8 Lucy _____ (hear) a strange noise.

9 The bat _____ (fly) near to the window.

10 Mina _____ (learn) how to type.

11 We _____ (can) see the lights from the ships.

B	F	L	E	W	N	U	S
S	U	T	C	O	U	L	D
O	T	O	S	K	U	D	E
W	R	O	T	E	D	L	Y
D	D	K	A	H	I	D	S
I	L	H	E	A	R	D	S
L	E	A	R	N	T	E	A
R	F	T	K	V	E	E	W
R	T	A	R	M	E	R	R

Vocabulary

2 In *Dracula*, we visit many different places. Match these places to the dictionary definitions below.

1 ☐ castle /ˈkɑːs(ə)l/   **a** a place where people catch a train
2 ☐ chapel /ˈtʃæp(ə)l/   **b** a very large church [people live(d) there]
3 ☐ abbey /ˈæbi/   **c** a place where ill people stay or live
4 ☐ hospital /ˈhɒspɪt(ə)l/   **d** a small church, sometimes private
5 ☐ hotel /həʊˈtel/   **e** a very, very large house, often on a hill
6 ☐ station /ˈsteɪʃ(ə)n/   **f** a place where tourists can stay

3a *Dracula* is a Gothic horror story. In Chapter One, we meet Jonathan Harker. He is travelling to Castle Dracula. Tick the adjectives you expect to read.

☐ beautiful   ☐ light
☐ dangerous   ☐ old
☐ dark   ☐ safe
☐ fat   ☐ small
☐ huge   ☐ thin
☐ modern   ☐ ugly

3b Write six pairs of opposites from the list of adjectives.

1 _____   _____
2 _____   _____
3 _____   _____
4 _____   _____
5 _____   _____
6 _____   _____

Chapter One

Count Dracula's Castle

▶ 2 *Jonathan Harker's Diary – 3ʳᵈ May, Bistritz*

I left Munich at 8.35 in the evening on 1st May and I arrived early the next morning. My train was an hour late, so I didn't have a lot of time to visit Budapest. But, it's a lovely place. The West meets the East here: some of the places in the town are almost Turkish. The bridges over the River Danube are beautiful.

The following morning, we left on time. We arrived in Klausenburgh late in the evening. I stayed the night at the Hotel Royal. I had an excellent dinner; chicken with hot red pepper. I asked the waiter about it. It's a national dish called *paprika hendl*. I must ask for the recipe. I want to give it to Mina.

I'm going to meet an important man. He lives in Castle Dracula. He's a count[1]. The castle is in the east of the country. It's between Transylvania, Moldavia and Bukovina. It's in the middle of the Carpathian Mountains. I'm going to his castle tomorrow. The count wants to buy a house in England. Mr Hawkins, my employer, has sent me here. We have found a large house for the count. It's in the village of Carfax. I have some drawings to show the count. I also took some photographs with my Kodak[2]. It's quite an old house, but Mr

1. **count:** 伯爵
2. **Kodak:** 這裏指一種照相機

Hawkins says it's perfect for the count. I hope Count Dracula likes it.

I didn't sleep very well after my dinner. My bed was comfortable, but I had a lot of strange dreams. A dog was howling[1] under my window. It howled for a lot of the night. I was also very thirsty, perhaps because of the paprika. I had more paprika for breakfast in a dish called *impletata*. It was also very good. I must ask for the recipe for this dish, too.

After breakfast, I went to the station. My train was at 8 o'clock and the journey was beautiful. We passed small towns, castles, hills and rivers. It was early evening when I arrived here, in Bistritz. An old lady at the Golden Krone hotel was expecting me. She gave me a letter from Count Dracula. It has directions for my journey tomorrow.

4th May

I'm writing this while I'm waiting for the coach[2]. The coach is going to take me to Count Dracula's castle. This morning, I asked the old lady and her husband about Count Dracula. I asked about his castle. They looked very frightened. They made the sign of a cross[3], several times. They said they didn't know anything. They didn't want to talk about it. A little later, the old lady came to speak to me, 'Do you have to go, Sir? Do you have to go? Tomorrow is St. George's Day. Tonight, at midnight, all the bad things in the world will happen. You don't understand. Don't go, Sir. Please wait until after St. George's Day.'

Then, she took a cross from her neck. 'For your mother,' she said and she put the cross around my neck. It was very strange. I must ask the count about it.

Ah! Here's the coach! Goodbye for now.

---

1. was howling: 吠叫 ▶KET◀
2. coach: 馬車

3. made the sign of a cross: 手劃十字

5th May – The Castle

I got on the coach and waited for the driver. He was talking to the old lady. They were talking about me. I didn't understand a lot of what they said, so I opened my little language dictionary. The words I heard didn't make me feel very happy. I heard *stregoica* – witch, then *vrolok* and *vlkoslak* – wolf[1] or vampire[2]! I must ask the count about this, too.

When the coach left, there were a lot of people at the coach station. They all made the sign of a cross. Then they pointed two fingers towards me. Again, I didn't feel very happy. I asked another passenger about this. He said that it was a sign against evil[3]. The people wanted to protect me. But why? I didn't understand.

This journey was also very beautiful. The fields were green and the apple trees and cherry trees were full of flowers. In the distance, we could see the snowy mountains. The coach driver drove very fast, but sometimes the road was difficult. 'These hills are difficult for the horses,' I said to the driver. 'At home, we usually walk if the horses have problems. Why don't we walk?'

But the driver didn't want us to walk. 'The dogs here are evil,' he said. 'It's too dangerous to walk.'

It began to get dark. The driver stopped for a moment. He lit[4] the lamps on the coach. Then, we started again. He was driving even more quickly. He seemed frightened of something. The horses seemed tired, but the driver didn't stop. He went faster and faster. We were getting near to my meeting place. The place where I had to meet Count Dracula's driver.

When we arrived, it was completely dark. There was no-one there. All the other passengers wanted me to stay on the coach.

1. wolf: 狼
2. vampire: 吸血鬼
3. evil: 邪惡
4. lit: 點亮

They wanted me to go to Bukovina. Then, there was a sound in the distance. It was the sound of horses. We could see lights, too. Count Dracula's coach was coming!

The count's driver got down from the coach. He was a tall man with a large black hat. His hat hid his face, but I could see his eyes. They looked red in the light from our lamps. He went towards our driver and said, 'Why are you so early? Did you want to miss me? Don't you want the gentleman to come with me?'

He smiled. It was a hard smile. He had very thin lips and very sharp[1] white teeth. Our driver seemed afraid and he didn't answer.

I got onto the count's coach. The count's driver helped me. I noticed that he was incredibly[2] strong. The four huge[3] black horses started off very fast. I was cold. I was also a little afraid. The driver put a coat over my shoulders and we went on, into the night. I looked at my watch in the light from the lamps. It was nearly midnight. In the distance, I heard a wolf howl. Then another, and another. It got louder and louder. I was afraid and the horses were afraid, too. The driver spoke to them and they calmed down. *He* wasn't afraid.

It got colder and colder. Snow started to fall. Suddenly, in the distance, I saw a blue light. The driver saw it, too. He got down from the coach and went towards the light. He held up his hand. The wolves were silent. Then, strangely, the wolves disappeared.

We drove on. Then, I saw it. The castle in the distance. Count Dracula's castle. The horses took us to the front of the castle. It was huge, dark and frightening.

The driver helped me down from the coach. Again, I noticed that he was very strong. He put my bags down next to me. Then, he

---

1. sharp: 尖銳的   **3. huge:** 龐大的
2. incredibly: 難以置信地

disappeared with the coach and horses. I was alone. I was alone in front of the huge castle door. I stood in silence and looked for a bell. I couldn't see one. I was frightened; I didn't know what to do. What kind of place was this? Where was I?

I waited and waited. It seemed like a very long time. Then I heard something. Someone was coming to the door. Slowly, the huge door opened. A tall man stood in front of me. He was holding a lamp. He had a long, white moustache and was very pale[1]. He was dressed completely in black. He spoke to me in excellent English, 'Welcome to my home. Please come in.'

Then he shook my hand[2]. His hands were incredibly strong. It almost hurt me. 'Count Dracula?' I asked.

'Yes, I am Dracula. Welcome to my home, Mr Harker. Come in. The night is cold and you are probably tired and hungry.'

Then he picked up my bags and I followed him. He took me up the stairs and along a long corridor. More stairs! Then along another corridor. The castle seemed dark and depressing[3]. At the end of the second corridor, he opened a huge door. 'Here. This is your room. I hope you will be comfortable.'

I was happy to see the room was full of light. There was a beautiful fire. 'Thank you. I'm sure I will be,' I said.

'Now, when you are ready, please come downstairs for supper.'

The count left me. I washed and I changed my clothes. Then, I went downstairs to have something to eat. The food was delicious. There was some chicken, some cheese and some salad. The count didn't eat anything. 'I had my supper before you arrived,' he said.

While I ate my supper, I looked at the count. He was tall, with

1. **pale:** 蒼白 ▶KET◀
2. **shook my hand:** 和我握手

3. **depressing:** 陰沉

a thin, sharp nose. He had a lot of hair on his head, but he also had hair on his hands. His face was pale and his lips were blood red. His teeth were very white and very sharp. Two of them were longer. These two teeth came over his lips. They looked like a dog's teeth. He looked very strange.

'And now you must go to bed,' said the count. 'Sleep for as long as you want.'

In the distance, we could hear the wolves howling.

'Listen to them. Listen to the music they make. They are like the children of the night!' said the count.

I was surprised. *I* didn't like the sound of the wolves.

7th May

I had a good day yesterday. I woke up late and went downstairs. Breakfast was ready. There was a note on the table.

I have to go away for some time today. Enjoy your breakfast. Do not wait for me – D.

After breakfast, I looked around the castle. It's a very strange place. A lot of the doors are locked[1]. It's very quiet. The only sounds I hear are the sounds of the wolves. In some rooms, there's some beautiful furniture and there are some beautiful pictures. In other rooms, some of the furniture is dirty and old. I haven't seen any servants[2]. Strangely, there are no mirrors in the castle. I used my small travel mirror to shave this morning.

This afternoon, I found a kind of library. I was very happy to find some English books in there. The count says I can use the library at any time. I can also go into any rooms in the castle, except the rooms which are locked.

1. **locked:** 上了鎖
2. **servants:** 僕人

In the evening, he asked me about the great house in Carfax. I told him about it. I showed him my Kodak photographs of it. It's not a very nice place. It's old and big and a little bit depressing. It has an old chapel[1] in the gardens. There's a psychiatric hospital nearby, but there aren't many houses. The count thinks that's a good thing. He doesn't like places which are full of people. He likes old places. He seems happy with it. I still think he's a very strange man. Again, we talked until late. Again, I had my supper alone. The count didn't eat with me.

8th May

I woke up late this morning. I seem to be living my life at night, not during the day. While I was shaving, the count came into my room. I was surprised, so I cut myself. I couldn't see him in my mirror! I turned around and he saw the blood on my face. He tried to attack[2] me. He seemed to want my blood! Then, his hand touched the cross on my neck. He stepped back. Almost immediately, he became calm. Then, he surprised me again. He took my mirror and threw it out of the window. It broke into a thousand pieces. Now, how am I going to shave?

I had my breakfast alone. The count wasn't there. It's strange, I have never seen him eat or drink. After breakfast, I looked around the castle some more. It's on the edge of a very high cliff[3]. Below it, there's a huge forest. More importantly, there isn't an exit. All the doors are locked. The only way out is through the very high windows. An impossible exit. It's a prison[4] and I'm a prisoner. I'm a prisoner here!

1. **chapel:** 小教堂
2. **attack:** 攻擊
3. **cliff:** 懸崖
4. **prison:** 監獄

Reading for KEY

1 Read Jonathan Harker's **first diary entry** again. Are the sentences right (A) or wrong (B)? Choose doesn't say (C), if there isn't enough information in the text to answer (A) or (B).

1 Jonathan left Munich in the morning.
A ☐ Right   B ☑ Wrong   C ☐ Doesn't say

2 Jonathan Harker thinks Budapest is beautiful.
A ☐ Right   B ☐ Wrong   C ☐ Doesn't say

3 Jonathan Harker had a room at the Hotel Royal.
A ☐ Right   B ☐ Wrong   C ☐ Doesn't say

4 Castle Dracula is very beautiful.
A ☐ Right   B ☐ Wrong   C ☐ Doesn't say

5 Mr Hawkins is Jonathan's employer.
A ☐ Right   B ☐ Wrong   C ☐ Doesn't say

6 In Bistritz, Jonathan gets a letter from Count Dracula.
A ☐ Right   B ☐ Wrong   C ☐ Doesn't say

Grammar

2a Questions. Put the words in the correct order to make questions about Dracula's Castle.

1 Count Dracula's/is/castle?/Where
_____*Where is Count Dracula's castle?*_____

2 there/Is/library?/a _____

3 go/Jonathan/all the rooms?/Can/into _____
_____

4 like/Jonathan/Does/his/room? _____

5 Jonathan/can/outside?/hear/What _____

6 do with/Count Dracula/does/Jonathan's mirror?/What
_____

2b Now answer your questions!

Vocabulary

3 **Geographical Features. Add the vowels (a,e,i,o,u) to complete the words. Then write the word next to the description below.**

1 m<u>o</u> <u>u</u>nt<u>a</u> <u>i</u>n
2 f_r_st
3 f_ _ld
4 h_ll
5 cl_ff
6 r_v_r

a ☐ Farmers grow things in one of these.   a _____ .
b ☐ Everest is a high one of these.   a _*mountain*_ .
c ☐ Count Dracula's castle is on one of these. a _____ .
d ☐ The Danube is one of these.   a _____ .
e ☐ There are lots of trees here.   a _____ .
f ☐ A small mountain.   a _____ .

PRE-READING ACTIVITY

Listening

▶ 3 **4a** **Listen to the next part of Jonathan Harker's diary. Are these statements true (T) or false (F)? Tick the correct box.**

	T	F
1 Jonathan is a prisoner in the castle.	✓	☐
2 The count has a lot of servants.	☐	☐
3 The count never talks to Jonathan.	☐	☐
4 The count is interested in history.	☐	☐
5 Count Dracula has a son called Attila.	☐	☐
6 Jonathan thinks the count is dangerous.	☐	☐
7 Jonathan has written to Mina.	☐	☐
8 Jonathan has a lot of bad dreams.	☐	☐

4b **Now read Chapter Two and check your answers.**

Chapter Two

The Horrible Dream

▶ 3 *Jonathan Harker's Diary (continued)*

There's no way out[1]! I'm a prisoner here! The count has made me a prisoner. But why?

Earlier today, I saw the count in my room. He was making my bed. Then, later, I saw him laying the table. This means he definitely doesn't have any servants. Does this mean that he was also the coach driver? The coach driver who brought me here? Does this mean that he can talk to wolves? Can he make wolves silent by holding up his hand? I'm feeling very afraid. Is this why the people of Bistritz didn't want me to come here? I must find out more about the count. But I must be careful.

Midnight

I talked to the count for a long time. I asked him about Transylvanian history. He likes to talk about history. He's very interesting about it. He loves to talk about war and blood. He talks about war like he was there at the time. He's related to Attila the Hun and he's very proud of it. I now think he's a dangerous man.

12th May

The count says I must stay here for a month. I've written to Mr Hawkins, my employer, to tell him the news. Count Dracula asked

---

1. **no way out:** 無路可逃

me to write. I also wrote to Mina. I didn't say anything about the count in my letters. I didn't say anything about being a prisoner. I gave my letters to the count. I'm sure he'll read them.

The count is busy again this evening. He's told me to be careful in the castle. He says I must be careful where I go. I must be careful where I sleep. I must only sleep in my own room. I must be careful not to fall asleep anywhere else. He says the castle is old; if I fall asleep in another room, I'll have bad dreams. Bad things can happen in this castle.

4   *Later*

When the count left me, I went to my room. I looked out of my window and I saw the count. He was climbing out of his window. Then he climbed down the cliff. He wasn't climbing like a man, he was climbing like an animal. Then, he disappeared into a gap[1] in the cliff!

15th May

Tonight, I saw the count go out of his window again. Again, he climbed down the cliff like an animal. I watched him go. I picked up my lamp. I went to look around the castle some more. This time, I went to new places. Places that I know the count goes. A lot of the doors were locked. Then, on one corridor, I found a door which wasn't locked. It was difficult to open, but I pushed it hard. The room inside was very light. There were no curtains at the window. The moon lit the room brightly. Now, here I am, in this room, writing my diary. I like this room more than my room. It doesn't feel like a prison.

Later: the Morning of 16th May

I finished writing my diary and put it in my pocket. Then I felt sleepy. I lay down on the sofa and went to sleep. I had a horrible dream. At least, I hope it was all a dream. It seems so real to me.

---

1. gap: 裂口

I was in the room, asleep. There were three young women. They came towards me. Two of them were dark. They looked very like the count. They had red eyes and long, sharp noses. The third was blonde. All three of them had very white teeth and very red lips. I thought their lips were beautiful. I wanted them to kiss me. Then, the blonde woman came towards me. She came to kiss me. She licked[1] her lips. She showed me her teeth. She had teeth like the count. Teeth like a dog. I could hear her breathing[2], near me. I could feel her teeth on my neck. I waited. Then, suddenly, I heard the count. He pulled the woman away. His eyes were on fire. He was very angry. He shouted at the women. 'Have that!' he said.

He threw a bag on the floor. Some*thing*, or some*one*, inside the bag cried.

I woke up in my own bed. Maybe it was a dream. Or maybe the count carried me here. My clothes are in the wardrobe, but not in their usual place. My watch has stopped. I usually check it before bed. There are other small things, too. But my diary is still here. It's still in my pocket. So perhaps it's my imagination.

19ᵗʰ May

I went down to look at the room in daylight. I want to know the truth. The door was locked from the inside. Now, I don't think it was a dream. I think the women wanted my blood.

I'm definitely in trouble. Last night the count asked me to write three letters. He told me to put different dates on them. He told me what to write. In one, I said that my work is nearly finished and that I'm coming home soon. In the second, I said that I'm leaving tomorrow. In the third letter, I said that I'm now at Bistritz. I dated the letters June 12ᵗʰ, June 19ᵗʰ and June 29ᵗʰ. Now I know. I must die before June 29ᵗʰ.

1. **licked:** 舔
2. **breathing:** 呼吸

28th May

There's a chance of escape. Some workers have come to the castle. They're camping outside. I must write some letters. Perhaps the workmen will post them for me.

I wrote two letters. One to Mr Hawkins and one to Mina. I wrote Mina's in shorthand[1]. I'm sure the count can't read shorthand. Then I put them around some money. I threw them to the workers. One of the workers took off his hat. He smiled.

Then, about five minutes later, the count came in. He was holding the letters. They were open. He looked at me. He was angry. Then, he threw the letters into the fire. He left the room and closed the door. He locked the door behind him. Now I'm a prisoner in my room, as well as in the castle. I went to bed. I was very tired.

31st May

This morning, I looked in my bag for paper and envelopes. They were missing. I looked in my wardrobe and my travelling clothes weren't there. My big coat is also missing. All my useful things are missing. All the things which are useful to me outside the castle. What's going to happen to me?

17th June

Earlier today, I was sitting on my bed. I heard a sound of horses outside. I looked out of my window. There was a team of horses there. They were pulling a cart[2]. There were a lot of long wooden boxes on the cart. Two workers were taking the boxes off the cart. The boxes looked like coffins[3]. Then the workers went away. Later they came back with more boxes.

---

1. shorthand: 速記
2. cart: 這裏指運貨馬車

3. coffins: 棺材

24th June, before morning

Last night, the count left me early. He went to his room and locked the door. I went to the window. I looked for him. After about half an hour, I saw the count. He was wearing *my* travelling clothes. He was carrying that horrible bag. He wants people to see *me* in the town. He wants people to see *me* posting letters. He wants people to see *me* doing bad things. Everyone is going to think *I* am bad.

Later, I woke up. I heard wolves howling. I heard the count in his room. I also heard someone crying in his room. Was it a child? Then I looked outside. There was a woman there. She saw me at the window. 'Give me my child. You monster! Give me my child,' she screamed[1]. She was crying. The count called out of his window. Suddenly, hundreds of wolves appeared. The woman screamed again. The wolves licked their lips. Then, they attacked her. Now, she was dead. Like her child.

25th June

I never see the count during the day. I always see him at night. Why is he always awake at night? Perhaps he sleeps during the day. I need to find some keys to the castle. Perhaps I can climb the cliffs like the count. Perhaps I can climb into his room. I'm going to try today.

Same day, later

I'm back in my room. I did it! I climbed into the count's room. It was empty. I looked for the keys. The keys to the castle and to the count's room. I didn't find them. Behind a door, there were some stairs. I went down the stairs. They were dark. They went outside. They went to a graveyard[2]. It was near an old chapel. In the graveyard, there were a lot of the wooden boxes. The same wooden boxes from

1. screamed: 尖叫
2. graveyard: 墓地

the cart. There were fifty of them. All of them were full of earth. I looked inside the boxes. In one of them, I saw the count. Was he dead? Was he asleep? It was impossible to say. His eyes were open, but he didn't look dead. His face wasn't cold, it was warm. His face was pale, but it was *always* pale. His lips were very red. I still didn't know; was he dead, or was he asleep? It was horrible. I ran back to the count's room. I climbed back to my room. I was very frightened.

29th June

29th June! The same date as my third letter. The last of the three letters the count told me to write. The count is going to England tomorrow. He says I can leave tomorrow too. But why can't I go *tonight*?

I asked the count. He opened the front door of the castle. 'Of course you can go,' he said. 'Go now!'

I looked out of the door. There were hundreds of wolves outside. They were howling at *me*. I couldn't leave.

Later, I heard the count. He was talking to the three women. 'Tomorrow! You will have everything tomorrow, my lovelies!' he said.

So, tomorrow is my last day. I must escape! I can't go tonight, but I'll try to climb down the cliffs tomorrow.

30th June, morning

This morning there's a lot of noise. The workers are putting the boxes onto carts. There are a lot of horses. The count is leaving. My room is locked. I'm a prisoner here. I must try to climb the cliffs.

Mina, I hope I see you again. If you find this diary, remember me. I love you very much.

★ ★ ★

Letter from Miss Mina Murray to Miss Lucy Westenra – 9ᵗʰ May

Dear Lucy,

How are you? I'm fine. I'm studying a lot at the moment. I'm learning to write in shorthand. I want to help Jonathan with his work. I'm also learning to use a typewriter¹. I'm now quite good. When Jonathan and I are married, I can type his work for him. I had a letter from him yesterday. He's coming back soon. He's writing a diary. I'm going to write a diary, too. A lot of people say it's very good for you. They say it helps your memory.

I'm really looking forward to seeing you. I've never been to Whitby, but I love the sea and I love the sea air.

Tell me everything, when you write to me. I haven't had any news from you for a long time. I've heard some stories about a tall, handsome man! Who is he? Write soon,

Love Mina

Letter from Lucy Westenra to Mina Murray – Wednesday

Dear Mina,

Thank you for your letter. Yes, you're right. There *is* a tall handsome man. His name's Mr Arthur Holmwood. We go out together sometimes. Sometimes, he comes to our house. Mother likes him a lot.

Oh, Mina, I think I love him. And, I think *he* loves *me*.

Please don't tell anyone. Write to me soon. You are my best friend in the world,

Love Lucy

---

1. **typewriter:** 打字機

Stop & Check

1 **Correct the mistakes in the letter from Lucy to Mina. There are seven mistakes.**

Dear Lucy,
How are you? I'm fine. I'm teaching a lot at the moment. I'm learning to write in German. I want to help Jonathan with his work. I'm also learning to use a computer. I'm now quite good. When Jonathan and I are married, I can type his work for him. I had a phone call from him yesterday. He's coming back soon. He's writing a book. I'm going to write one, too. A lot of people say it's very good for you. They say it helps your memory.
I'm really looking forward to seeing you. I've often been to Whitby. I love the sea and I love the sea air.
Tell me everything, when you write to me. I haven't had any news from you for a long time. I've heard some stories about a short, handsome man! Who is he? Write soon,
Love Mina

Vocabulary

2a **Solve the anagrams to find the parts of the body. The first letter is there to help you.**

acef	f _ _ _	adeh	h _ _ _
eetth	t _ _ _ _	ilps	l _ _ _
cekn	n _ _ _	aers	e _ _ _
enos	n _ _ _	eesy	e _ _ _

2b **Which adjectives can you use to describe the parts of the body above? Use the words in the box.**

> sharp • red • long • white

Vocabulary

3a Match the adjectives from box A with their opposites from box B.

A	B
1 silent	**a** boring
2 interesting	**b** useless
3 light	**c** dark
4 useful	**d** safe
5 dangerous	**e** noisy

3b Choose an adjective from 3a to fill the sentences below.

1 Count Dracula finds Transylvanian history very _____.

2 When the count holds up his hand, wolves are _____.

3 Jonathan thinks that the count is a very _____ man.

4 Count Dracula's room is very _____, there are no curtains.

PRE-READING ACTIVITY

Listening

▶ 5 **4** Listen to the letters from the beginning of Chapter Three. Tick A, B, or C. Listen twice.

1 Who is the first letter from?

A ☑ Lucy Westenra   **B** ☐ Mina Murray   **C** ☐ John Seward

2 How many men want to marry Lucy?

A ☐ one   **B** ☐ two   **C** ☐ three

3 How old is Dr Seward?

A ☐ 24   **B** ☐ 29   **C** ☐ 25

4 Where is the second man from?

A ☐ Murray   **B** ☐ Texas   **C** ☐ the hospital

5 Lucy is going to marry

A ☐ John   **B** ☐ Quincey   **C** ☐ Arthur

6 How old is R.M. Renfield?

A ☐ 29   **B** ☐ 49   **C** ☐ 59

Chapter Three

Renfield's Pets

▶ 5 *Letter from Lucy Westenra to Mina Murray – 24th May*

Thank you and thank you again for your lovely letter. Now, I have more news for you. Today has been a fantastic day. Three men asked me to marry them. Yes, three! And all on the same day. I feel very sorry for two of them. Mina, I'm *so* happy. Please don't tell anyone. But of course, you can tell Jonathan.

Number one was Dr John Seward. A few months ago, Arthur introduced me to him. He's very clever and very interesting. He's only 29 years old and he's already an important doctor. He's the head doctor in a psychiatric hospital. I like him very much. But I don't love him. We have decided to stay friends.

Number two came just after lunch. He's a man from Texas. His name's Mr Quincey P. Morris. He's a very nice man. He's also a friend of Arthur's. But, I'm sorry. I said no to him, too. He was sad, but very kind.

Then came number three. I don't need to tell you about *him*. Yes, Mina, it's Arthur! Arthur wants to marry me. I'm so happy! I hope he will still be friends with John and Quincey. They're all very nice men.

I don't want him to lose his friends. But Mina, I'm so, so happy,

Love Lucy

Dr John Seward's Diary (recorded on phonograph[1]) – 25th May

I'm sad today. Yesterday, I asked Lucy to marry me. She said no. I have decided to think about my work. That usually helps. So, I went to see some of the patients. There's one patient who's very interesting: Name – R. M. Renfield. Age – 59. Sometimes calm. Sometimes angry. Sometimes depressed. Very, very strong. Possibly dangerous.

I must talk to him more. I want to find out more about him.

Mina Murray's Diary – 24th July – Whitby

Lucy came to meet me at the station. Whitby is a lovely town, by the sea. There's an old abbey[2] at the top of the hill. Next to the abbey, is a graveyard. It's on a cliff. There are some wonderful views up there. People often go up there to walk. Lucy and I went for a walk there, this afternoon. There are some lovely walks along the cliffs. You can sit there, too and watch the ships in the harbour[3].

1st August

We went up to the abbey again today. We sat in the graveyard and looked at the view. Lucy talked a lot about Arthur. She talked about her wedding. I'm happy for her, but I was also a little sad. I haven't heard anything from Jonathan for almost a month.

Later, I went up to the graveyard alone. I could see the lights from the ships. I thought about Jonathan. I hope he's well and nothing has happened. I want to see him. I miss him.

1. phonograph: 留聲機
2. abbey: 修道院
3. harbour: 港口

Dr Seward's Diary – 5ᵗʰ June

Renfield is a very interesting patient. He has the look of a killer in his eyes. But he has a good quality; he likes animals. At the moment, he likes flies. The flies are his pets. He's got a lot. He gives them sugar and they come to him. I think that there are too many.

18ᵗʰ June

Now Renfield likes spiders. So, spiders are his new pets. He gives the flies to the spiders. The spiders eat them. There aren't many flies left now.

1ˢᵗ July

Renfield has now got a lot of spiders. He has got a notebook, where he writes lots of notes. I think they're notes about the spiders.

8ᵗʰ July

Now, he has a new pet. He's got a little bird. There are not so many spiders now. He gives the spiders to the bird. The bird eats them.

19ᵗʰ July

Renfield has now got a lot of birds. They come to him for food. I went to see him. He was very pleased to see me. He asked me for something. 'I want a kitten,' he said. 'I want a kitten that I can feed and feed and feed.'

I was ready for this. First, he had some flies. Then, he had some spiders. His spiders ate the flies. Then, he had some birds. His birds ate the spiders. Now, he wants a cat. I understood his plan. 'I will think about it,' I said to him. He looked at me. He was angry. He's an interesting patient.

Evening

I went to see Renfield again. He was crying. He asked me again

1. **pets:** 寵物 ▶KET◀

and again, 'Can I have a kitten? Please, please, please!'

I said no.

20th July

I went to see him this morning. He was happy. He was giving sugar to flies again. There weren't any birds in his room. But there was some blood. He says the birds have gone away. I think he has eaten them. He's definitely[1] a killer. He needs my help.

Mina Murray's Diary – 26th July

I'm very worried. Lucy isn't sleeping very well. She's walking in her sleep. Tonight I'm locking the door. I don't want her to hurt herself. Her mother, Mrs Westenra, thinks this is a good idea.

3rd August

There's still no news from Jonathan. I looked at his last letter. It's a little strange. It's in his writing, but he seems very formal. I hope he isn't ill. I hope he's alright.

I'm not sleeping very well, because Lucy is still walking in her sleep. She gets out of bed, then she goes to the door. When she finds it's locked, she goes to look for the key. I'm worried about her.

6th August

The weather is very stormy today. Lucy and I went up to the cliff. The fishing boats were all coming home before the storm. A kind old man came to talk to us. His name's Mr Sales. He was once a sailor. We all saw a ship in the distance. The old man thinks it's an empty ship. He can see by the way it moves in the wind. He says the ship will probably come to the harbour tomorrow. The storm will bring it.

1. **definitely:** 毫無疑問

Reports from The Dailygraph newspaper – from Mina Harker's diary

8th August – Whitby – Report by George White

WHITBY STORM MYSTERY!

During last night's terrible storm in Whitby, a Russian ship, the *Demeter*, came into the harbour. The captain of the ship was dead. He had a cross in his hand. There was no-one else on the ship. People saw a huge dog. It jumped off the ship and ran up the hill to the graveyard. Local people have tried to find the dog. They want to give it food.

9th August – Whitby – Report by George White

RUSSIAN CAPTAIN'S DIARY FOUND!

The Russian ship, the *Demeter*, is carrying fifty wooden boxes. They are full of earth, for scientific research. A Whitby lawyer, Mr Billington, has instructions to send them to a house in the village of Carfax.

No-one has seen the huge dog.

A translation of the captain's diary follows:

14th July – The sailors are afraid. They say that there's *something* on the ship. Then they make the sign of a cross.

19th July – Petrofsky is missing. Olgaren says there's a strange man on the ship.

26th July – Another sailor disappeared today. The other men are all frightened. I have my gun with me. We can't find the strange man.

30th July – There are only four of us on the ship now. I don't understand what's happening.

3rd August – There was a cry in the night. I went to look outside. There was no-one at the wheel. I have searched the ship. I'm alone. I'm the captain, I must stay with my ship. Help me God!

The next page was blank. What happened on the *Demeter*? We demand[1] to know.

1. demand: 要求

10th August – Whitby – Report by George White

DEAD DOGS ON BAKER'S FARM

Another Whitby mystery. Who, or what, killed the dogs on Baker's farm? William Baker found his dogs this morning. They were covered in blood. Is Whitby safe?

Mina Murray's Diary – 8th August

Lucy didn't sleep very well last night. She got up twice and got dressed. I put her back to bed. I think the storm disturbed her.

This morning, we went down to the harbour together. It was a beautiful day. The air was clear and fresh. The old sailor was right. The empty ship was in the harbour. The poor captain was dead. Some people saw a huge dog. It ran off the boat. Lucy and I tried to find it. We wanted to give it some food and water. We couldn't find it.

10th August

It was the poor captain's funeral[1] today. Some of the sea captains from the harbour carried the coffin up the hill. All the sailors followed. My kind old sailor, Mr Sales, wasn't there. He died this morning, too. They found him by our favourite seat, near the abbey. He had a broken neck. People say he looked frightened. What happened to him?

I want Lucy to sleep well tonight. We're going to go for a long walk. Then she'll be tired and she'll sleep.

11th August, 3 a.m.

I can't sleep now, I'm too worried. I woke up at about 1 o'clock. Lucy wasn't here. I went downstairs to look for her. The front door was open. I ran outside and looked in the street. There was no-one

---

1. funeral: 葬禮

there. I looked for her everywhere. Then I thought about the abbey and our favourite seat. I began to climb the hill. Then I saw her. She was lying on our seat. Was she sleeping? There was a man near her. 'Lucy! Lucy!' I shouted. She didn't answer. The man looked up and I saw a very white face and red eyes. Then he ran away.

Lucy was still sleeping, but she looked cold. I put my coat around her neck, but I think I hurt her. I saw a little blood on her neck. There were two small marks[1] there. Then, I woke her up. I carefully took her home. I put her to bed. I locked the door and have the key around my wrist.

Same day, much later, night-time

I woke Lucy in the morning. She didn't look tired after her busy night. She looked very well. We had a happy day together. We had a picnic by the sea with Mrs Westenra. I'm sad that Jonathan isn't here. I miss him very much. Again, I've locked the door of our room. The key is around my wrist. But I don't think there'll be any problems tonight.

12ᵗʰ August

I was wrong. Lucy got up twice in the night. She was asleep, but she seemed very worried that the door was locked. Both times, she went back to bed, but she was almost angry.

---

1. **marks:** 這裏指血污 ▶KET◀

AFTER-READING ACTIVITIES

Stop & Check

1 **Put the events from Chapter Three in the order they appear in the text.**

☐ Mina puts a key around her wrist.
☐ Mina arrives in Whitby.
☐ Mr Sales dies.
☐ Renfield has got a lot of birds.
☐ There's a storm at sea.
☐ John Seward asks Lucy to marry him.
☐ A ship arrives at the harbour in Whitby.
☐ Renfield has got a lot of spiders.

Writing for KEY

2a **Complete Lucy's postcard to Arthur. Write ONE word for each space.**

Dearest Arthur,

Mina and I (**1**) _are_ having a wonderful time. I'm very happy that she (**2**) _____ come to visit me. We (**3**) _____ for walks every day on the hill, near the abbey. There are (**4**) _____ lovely walks along the cliffs. We often sit there and watch the ships (**5**) _____ the harbour.

I have (**6**) _____ of plans for our wedding! When are you coming (**7**) _____ visit me?

Write and let me know as (**8**) _____ as possible!

Your Lucy

2b **Write a postcard to your friend in London. Say what you did yesterday.**

Writing

3a Message in a Bottle. The Captain of the *Demeter* wrote a message in code. Use the key to crack the code.

ZITKT OL Q LZKQFUT DQF GF DN LIOH. VT FTTR ITSH

Q = A	W = B	E = C	R = D	T = E	Y = F	U = G	I = H
O = I	P = J	A = K	S = L	D = M	F = N	G = O	H = P
J = Q	K = R	L = S	Z = T	X = U	C = V	V = W	B = X
N = Y	M = Z						

3b Can you work out how the code was made? The coded message below has the answer.

This code - XLTL ZIT ATNL OF ZIT GKRTK ZITN QKT GF Q ATNWGQKR

3c Work in pairs. Use the code. Write your own coded message for your partner.

_____

_____

PRE-READING ACTIVITY

Speaking

4 Look at the picture on page 33. Dr Seward is recording his notes onto a phonograph (one of the first recording machines). Work in pairs. Ask your partner questions about these modern gadgets.

mobile phone • computer • tablet • television • gaming console

1 Have you got a _____?
2 Do you like your _____? Why/Why not?
3 Would you like a new _____?
4 Is your _____ old or new?
5 What's your favourite gadget? _____

Chapter Four

The Marks on her Neck

▶ 1 *Mina Murray's Diary (continued) – 13th August*
Another quiet day. Lucy is looking very well. I'm happy she's herself again. Again, she woke me up in the night. This time she was sitting in bed. She was still asleep, but she was pointing to the window. I went to the window and opened the curtains. It was very light outside, because the moon was very bright. It was beautiful to see the light on the sea. There was also a large bat in the distance. Once or twice, it came quite near to the window. Then it flew away across the harbour and up to the abbey. Perhaps I frightened it. I went back to bed. Lucy was lying down again and sleeping very quietly.

14th August

We went up to our cliff again today. We were reading and writing all day. Lucy loves it so much, sometimes she doesn't want to come home. Today, when we were coming home, she said a strange thing. 'His eyes. His red eyes again. They're the same.'

I was surprised and I looked at her. She wasn't asleep, but she looked like she was dreaming. She was looking at our favourite seat. I wasn't sure. Was someone sitting there?

Later, after Lucy was in bed, I went for a walk. It was a beautiful evening. I went to the harbour and looked at the sea. On my way home, I saw Lucy at the bedroom window. The window was open and she was looking out. I think there was a large bird next to her. Then I saw that she was asleep. I came upstairs quickly. I didn't want her to get cold. When I came into the room, Lucy was already in bed. The bird wasn't there. Lucy was holding her neck. I think she was cold. I'm worried, I hope she isn't ill. I closed the window carefully and locked the door again.

15th August

We had a happy surprise at breakfast. Arthur's father is better. He wants Lucy and Arthur to get married soon. Mrs Westenra is happy, but sad, too. She's ill: she's got a problem with her heart. Her doctor says she must be careful. She's very weak[1] and a sudden shock[2] could kill her. I'm sorry. Lucy knows that her mother is ill, but she doesn't know that it's so serious. I've promised[3] not to tell Lucy.

17th August

Lucy is tired and very weak. She's still walking in her sleep. Her face is very pale. The marks on her neck are still there. They aren't any better. I'm worried that she's ill. Tonight, I woke up and she was sitting by the window again. I went to close the window and she went back to bed. She was breathing very strangely. I think I'll ask the doctor to come. I'm very worried about her.

18th August

I'm happy today. Lucy is much better. She slept well last night and didn't walk in her sleep. She has some colour in her face, but she's still pale. We went up to our seat and looked at the view. We talked and

1. **weak:** 虛弱
2. **shock:** 震驚

3. **promised:** 答應

talked. Lucy talked about *that* night. She said it wasn't a dream, but she saw something with red eyes. She said she saw me *before* I woke her up. It was very strange. I didn't want her to talk about it any more. So we talked about other things. We talked and laughed. More and more colour came into her face. When we came home, Mrs Westenra was very happy; she agrees with me. Lucy looks much better.

19ᵗʰ August

I'm so, so happy! News from Jonathan. I'm happy, but I'm sad too. He's been very ill. That's why he didn't write to me. I got a letter this morning from a nurse. Her name's Sister Agatha and she works in a hospital in Budapest. Jonathan was too ill to write, but wanted to send me a letter. She wrote the letter for him. He wants to see me. He loves me and misses me. I'm leaving as soon as possible. Lucy is going to send my things home. I can't wait to see him.

Letter from Mina Harker to Lucy Westenra – Budapest 24ᵗʰ August

Dear Lucy,

Here I am in Budapest. I'm with my Jonathan. He's pale and ill, but it's lovely to see him. Now I can be his nurse. He doesn't remember a lot of things. Sister Agatha says that he's shocked. Perhaps he'll never remember. She says that he talked of terrible things in his sleep. I asked her about them, but she won't tell me. She says that they're Jonathan's secrets with God. She's a very good person.

Jonathan doesn't remember what happened to him. He gave me his notebook. He wrote everything in shorthand. He doesn't want to read it himself. He doesn't want to remember things. He says I must

read it, if I want to. I put the book under his pillow[1]. I don't want to read it now. I'll only read it, if Jonathan asks me to.

The most important news: we're getting married this afternoon. I'm going to be Mrs Mina Harker. Lucy, I'm so happy,

Love Mina

Letter from Lucy Westenra to Mina Harker – Whitby 30th August
Dear Mina,

I hope you can come home soon with Jonathan. The air here is very good. I'm sure it'll be good for him. I'm feeling much better. Arthur is here and we're having a wonderful time. I'm not walking in my sleep at all, at the moment. Arthur and I are getting married on 28th September. I'm so happy.

Mother hopes you're well. She sends her love,
Love Lucy

Dr Seward's Diary – 20th August
Renfield is often very violent[2] during the day. Then he's very quiet at night. He has escaped three times in three nights. Each time, he goes to the door of the chapel at the great house in Carfax. He doesn't do anything there. He just stays there, with his face against the door. Tonight, we found him there again. He was talking to someone. He said, 'I'm here, Master. I'm here for you.'

Then he calmed down. He was looking at a big bat in the sky. He was smiling: he seemed to like the bat. We took him back to the hospital. I hope I can help him.

1. **pillow:** 枕頭
2. **violent:** 暴躁

Letter from Arthur Holmwood to Dr Seward – 31ˢᵗ August
Dear John,

I'm worried[1] about Lucy. I think she's ill. She's getting paler every day. Her friend Mina was worried about her. Now I'm worried too. I must go to my father. He's very ill again, but I really need your help.

Can you come and see her soon?

Your friend,

Arthur

Dr Seward's Diary – 1ˢᵗ September
Today, I went to see Lucy Westenra. Arthur is right. There *is* something wrong. She's very pale and looks very weak. I don't know what's wrong with her. I'm going to write to my old teacher, my good friend, Professor Van Helsing. I'm sure he can help us. He knows a lot about people who walk in their sleep.

I hope he understands my letter. He's from Holland and sometimes he has problems with his English.

Letter from Professor Van Helsing to Dr Seward
My dear friend,

Does not worry. I is coming to you. I does can help you,

Van H.

Letter from Dr Seward to Arthur Holmwood – 3ʳᵈ September
Dear Arthur,

The professor came today. He agrees with us. Lucy is ill. She's very pale. She doesn't have enough blood. That's what the professor

---

1. worried: 擔心 ▶KET◀

thinks. He isn't sure what the problem is, but he has an idea. He's going back to Amsterdam tomorrow to do some research.

How's your father? I hope he's getting better.

Your friend,

John

Dr Seward's Diary – 4th September

Renfield was very violent yesterday. Now he's calm and back in his room. He's catching flies again. First he was eating them, now he's putting them in a box. He's already looking for a spider. He asked me for more sugar.

I went to see Lucy this afternoon. She's looking better. When I came back, Renfield was angry again. He was shouting and screaming. Then, when the sun went down, he calmed down again. He did a strange thing. He went to his window and threw away his flies. I asked him about it. He said he was bored with them. He's a very interesting patient. When he's violent, it's never at night. It's always during the day.

Telegram[1] from Dr Seward to Professor Van Helsing – 6th September

COME AT ONCE. LUCY IS VERY ILL.

---

1. telegram: 電報

Stop & Check

1 **Answer the questions about Chapter Four.**

1 Is Mina worried about Lucy?
Yes, she is.

2 Is Arthur's father better?

3 Is Lucy's mother ill?

4 Does Mina get some news from Jonathan?

5 Are Lucy and Arthur already married?

6 Is Professor Van Helsing from Holland?

7 Does Renfield like flies and spiders?

Grammar

2 **Modal Verbs. Professor Van Helsing often makes mistakes with his English. Use a red pen. Correct the mistakes he has made in this letter.**

My dear friend,

You don't must worry. I am coming to England immediately.
Can you to pick me up at the station in Carfax? I will to arrive
at 8 pm. I don't will be late. I do can help you. Do I can stay
with you at the hospital?

Your friend

Van Helsing

Speaking for KEY

3a Here is some information about a holiday. Use the words to write questions about the information.

TWO NIGHTS IN BUDAPEST □ 250

Leave London Airport: 26th July
Visit all the tourist attractions
Accommodation: in a four star hotel

For more information visit www.budapestbreak.com

---

1 where? ___*Where is the holiday to?*___
2 how much/cost? _____
3 where/stay? _____
4 when/leave? _____
5 what/do? _____
6 website? _____

3b Work in pairs. Ask and answer your questions.

PRE-READING ACTIVITY

Listening

4a Listen to the first part of Chapter Five. Circle the correct answer.

1 Lucy was (pale)/dark.
2 Lucy was better/worse than yesterday.
3 Her breathing was very bad/good.
4 Arthur's father is a little worse/better.
5 Arthur got paler and paler/darker and darker.
6 The marks on her neck were black/red.

4b Now read the text and check your answers.

Chapter Five

The Wrong Address

▶ 8 *Dr Seward's Diary – 7*[th] *September*
Professor Van Helsing and I went to see Lucy today. She was very, very pale. Even worse than yesterday. Her face was white. Even her lips were white. Her breathing was very weak again. The professor said she needs blood. Lots of blood.

Arthur arrived. His father is a little better. The professor asked Arthur to give his blood to Lucy. We went up to Lucy's room. The professor took some things from his bag. He gave Lucy something to help her sleep. Arthur kissed her. Then the professor gave Arthur's blood to Lucy. The colour started to come back to her face. Arthur became paler and paler.

Lucy wears a black band[1] around her neck, with a beautiful diamond in the centre. The diamond was a present from Arthur. When the professor touched Lucy's head, the band moved a little. Both the professor and I saw two small marks on her neck. They were quite red. The professor seemed shocked and very worried. Arthur didn't see the marks. I took him back to his room. He needed to rest. ■

▶ 9 When I came back into Lucy's room, the band was covering her neck again. I asked the professor about the marks. He couldn't tell me

1. **band:** 細帶子

about them. He's going back to Amsterdam tonight. He says there are books there that he needs. He says I must stay with Lucy all night. I mustn't leave her. He says I mustn't sleep. I must watch her all night.

10th September

I stayed awake with Lucy for two nights. At first, she didn't want to sleep. She was afraid. Then, I promised to stay with her and to wake her up, if she had a bad dream. Both nights, she slept very well. Yesterday, she looked much better. I was very, very tired last night. Lucy told me to sleep. It was a good idea. I slept on the sofa in her room.

This morning, I woke up when the professor came into the room. I opened the curtains and the light came into the room. Lucy didn't wake up. She was white – whiter than white. There wasn't any time. She needed blood. This time, I gave her my blood. When she woke up, she looked better. The professor told me to go home. He told me to sleep. He's going to look after Lucy.

11th September

This morning, I went to see Lucy. She's much better. While I was there, some flowers arrived. The professor took them to Lucy. I helped him to put the flowers around her room. Then we made a necklace of flowers for her. The flowers don't smell very nice: they're garlic[1] flowers. The professor says they're Lucy's medicine. She doesn't like them very much. She wants to get better, so she's wearing them. I think it's a very strange medicine, but I trust the professor. He knows what he's doing. He told Lucy not to open the door or the window of her room. Then we left. He says we can sleep well tonight. Nothing will happen to Lucy. He's sure.

---

1. **garlic:** 大蒜 ▶KET◀

13th September

The professor and I went to see Lucy this morning. When we arrived, Mrs Westenra came to meet us. 'You'll be happy to know, Lucy's better. I went to her room a short time ago. She's still sleeping. I went to her room in the night. I was worried about her. She was sleeping well, but the room smelled horrible. I took away those horrible flowers and I opened the window. It smells much better now.'

At this news, the professor went white. Mrs Westenra went away. Then the professor put his head in his hands and cried, 'What has the lady done? What has she done? What has she done?' he said, again and again.

We ran upstairs[1] to Lucy's room. She was very, very ill. This time, the professor gave his blood to Lucy. 'You are not strong. You gave your blood last time,' he said. 'Now you must help me. Help me to give my blood to her.'

Then we put flowers around the room again. We closed the window and left Lucy. She was sleeping quietly and she looked better. We went downstairs[2] to see Mrs Westenra. The professor talked to her about the flowers. 'The flowers are a medicine, Mrs Westenra. You must not take them away. They must stay in the room. Please remember. They must stay.'

Then I left. I hope Lucy will be alright. She seems calmer when she has the flowers with her. The professor is going to stay with her.

17th September

I was in my study after dinner, when I had a shock. Renfield ran into my room. I don't know how he got out of his room. I must ask the nurses. He had a knife in his hand and he attacked me. He cut my

---

1. **upstairs:** 樓上 ▶KET◀
2. **downstairs:** 樓下 ▶KET◀

wrist. There was quite a lot of blood. When he saw the blood on the floor, he calmed down. Then he lay on the floor and tried to drink the blood, like an animal. It was horrible to see. The nurses ran in. They picked him up and took him to his room. He was still calm, but he wanted more blood.

18th September

I got a telegram from the professor this morning. It arrived very late, because he put the wrong address on it.

Telegram from Professor Van Helsing in Amsterdam, to Dr Seward in Carfax, 17th September

I AM IN HOLLAND. GO TO LUCY'S HOUSE TONIGHT. WATCH HER.
DO NOT LEAVE HER ALONE.

I'm very worried. The telegram was a day late. Lucy was alone last night, I must go to her immediately.

Note from Lucy Westenra – 17th September

I'm writing this because I don't know what to do. I'm alone and I'm frightened.

Last night, I went to bed as usual. I put the flowers all around my room. In the middle of the night, I woke up. There was a noise at my window. I looked out and saw the huge bat again. Then in the distance, I heard a dog howling. The noise got louder and louder. I tried to go back to sleep, but I was afraid. Then Mother came into my room. She said she was worried about me. Then we heard the noise at the window and she saw the bat. She looked frightened and a little shocked. I told her to sit down. I didn't want her to be ill. I could hear her heart.

1. wrist: 手腕

After a while, we heard the howling noise again. This time, it sounded very near. Suddenly, there was a loud noise at the window. A lot of broken glass fell on the floor. Then, there, in the middle of the room, we saw a large wolf. We both screamed. Mother jumped up and tried to hold onto me. She pulled the flowers from my neck and then fell onto the floor, on top of me. I hit my head. The room seemed to go around[1] in circles. The room was full of strange blue lights. Then the wolf went away. I couldn't move: my mother was on top of me. The servants ran into the room. They lifted my mother up; she was dead. They put her on the bed. They were all very frightened. I told them to go away. I told them to get some tea and to calm down. I put my flowers on my mother's body. Then I waited for one of the servants to come back. No-one came. I called out. Still no-one came. I went to the kitchen to find them. They were all asleep on the floor. I looked around the kitchen. I found a small bottle of medicine. It was empty. It is – oh! *was!* – my mother's medicine. It helped her to sleep. I smelled the tea in the servants' cups. I could smell the medicine.

Now I'm back in my room with Mother. I'm alone. Alone with the dead. I can hear the wolf; it's howling outside. I can see the blue lights all around my room. I'm very frightened. I think I'm going to die. I'm going to put this note in my pocket. Someone will find it when I die.

Goodbye, dear Arthur. I love you.

Dr Seward's Diary – 18th September
I went to Lucy's house immediately. When I arrived, it was 10 o'clock in the morning. I knocked at the door, but no-one came. I tried all the doors and windows. They were all locked. Then I heard

1. go around: 旋轉

someone behind me: it was the professor. When he saw me, he was very shocked. 'Did you get my telegram? Why are you here? Where's Lucy?'

I told him everything. He went very pale. He tried all the doors and windows, too. Then he said, 'We must get inside. We must break a window.'

We broke one of the kitchen windows and climbed inside. We saw the servants on the floor. We ran up to Lucy's bedroom. There, we saw the two women. Lucy was lying next to her dead mother. She was cold, but she was breathing. Lucy was alive[1]! We took her to another room. A note fell out of her pocket. We put her in bed and covered her up. She began to get warmer. The professor looked very worried. 'She must have blood. You are too tired. You can't give more blood. I am too tired. But she must have blood. She must have blood again.'

Then, there was a voice at the door. 'Can I help? Can I give my blood to dear Lucy?'

It was my old friend, Quincey Morris! He had a telegram from Arthur with him.

QUINCEY, GO TO LUCY'S HOUSE. NO NEWS FROM SEWARD. FATHER IS VERY ILL. I CAN'T GO MYSELF. PLEASE GO TO LUCY. SEE IF SHE IS ALRIGHT. ARTHUR.

It was good to see Quincey. And it was good he was here; Quincey was strong. He gave his blood to Lucy. Then, the professor gave me Lucy's note. I read it and gave it back to him. It seems a mad note to me, but the professor is worried. He doesn't think Lucy is mad. He put the note back in Lucy's pocket. Then, he took the band off Lucy's

1. **alive:** 活着

neck. The marks are still there; they almost look bigger. He covered the marks with a scarf[1].

Quincey and I went to talk. I told him everything. He's going to help us. He's going to sit with Lucy, too. He's going to watch her.

19th September

Last night, Lucy slept badly. She had some bad dreams. When she woke up, she was very ill. It's strange, but when she's awake, her breathing is very weak. When she's asleep, it's better. Another strange thing is her teeth. Perhaps it's only the evening light, but when she's asleep, two of her teeth look longer.

She wanted to see Arthur, so we sent a telegram. Quincey went to meet him at the station. Lucy was very happy to see him. She looked a little better, but she's still very ill.

It's now nearly midnight. Arthur and the professor are sitting with her. I'm going to sit with her at 1 o'clock. Then the others can sleep. I'm very worried about her. I don't think she's going to get better. I'm worried that she's going to die.

1. scarf: 圍巾

Stop & Check

1 Match the questions and answers.

1 $\boxed{e}$ What did Arthur give to Lucy?
2 ☐ Why did the professor go back to Amsterdam?
3 ☐ How many nights did Dr Seward stay awake for?
4 ☐ What did the professor put in Lucy's room?
5 ☐ What did Mrs Westenra do?
6 ☐ What did Renfield do to Dr Seward?
7 ☐ Why did the telegram arrive late?
8 ☐ Why did Lucy and Mrs Westenra scream?

a Two.
b The address was wrong.
c He put some garlic flowers there.
d A wolf jumped into Lucy's room.
e He gave his blood to her.
f She took the garlic flowers away.
g He wanted to look at some books.
h He attacked him.

Vocabulary

2a Read the description of some jobs from _Dracula_. Guess the word. The first letter is already there.

1 Someone who cleans the house for you. s _e_ _r_ _v_ _a_ _n_ _t_
2 Someone who visits you when you are ill. d _ _ _ _ _ _
3 Someone who works in a hospital. n _ _ _ _
4 Someone who works for a newspaper. r _ _ _ _ _ _ _
5 Someone who teaches at a university. p _ _ _ _ _ _ _ _
6 Someone who helps with legal problems. l _ _ _ _ _

2b Which of these jobs would you most/least like to do?

Reading for KEY

3 **Read the sentences about a reporter's day. Choose the best word (A, B, or C) for each space.**

1 George White ___*writes*___ for the *Dailygraph*.
   A ☐ sings   **B** ☐ writes   **C** ☐ reads

2 George _____ at work at 9.30 am.
   A ☐ arrives   **B** ☐ gets   **C** ☐ goes

3 He usually _____ a coffee in a café at 10 am.
   A ☐ buys   **B** ☐ pays   **C** ☐ spends

4 He _____ to people about stories for his newspaper.
   A ☐ phones   **B** ☐ talks   **C** ☐ asks

5 George has to _____ his articles.
   A ☐ draw   **B** ☐ speak   **C** ☐ type

6 George would really _____ to work for a national newspaper.
   A ☐ like   **B** ☐ want   **C** ☐ hope

PRE-READING ACTIVITY

Speaking

4 **There are a lot of dramatic events in Chapter Six. What do you think happens? Choose A or B and discuss your answers with your partner.**

1 **A** Lucy gets better.
   B Lucy dies.

2 **A** Seward sees Count Dracula in London.
   B Jonathan sees Count Dracula in London.

3 **A** Count Dracula attacks children.
   B Lucy attacks children.

Chapter Six

The Bloofer Lady

▶ 10 *Dr Seward's Diary (continued) – 20th September*

What a terrible few days. Lucy's mother. Then Arthur's father. And now … yes, now Lucy.

I sat with her all night until 6 o'clock. Then the professor came in and opened the curtains. She was very, very pale and her breathing was terrible. He took the scarf off her neck. He was obviously worried, so I went to look at Lucy. Where were the marks? The marks on her neck weren't there any more. The professor looked at me. 'She's dying. Bring Arthur here. He must see her.'

I brought Arthur into the room and Lucy smiled at him. He smiled, too and went to kiss her. 'No. Not now,' said the Professor. 'Hold her hand. You can kiss her later.'

He held her hand and she went to sleep. A short time later, her breathing was better. She opened her mouth a little. Again, two of her teeth seemed longer. She opened her eyes and spoke; her voice was very strange. 'Kiss me, Arthur. Kiss me.'

Arthur went to kiss her, but the professor stopped him. 'NO ARTHUR! NO!' he shouted. And he pulled Arthur away from Lucy.

Arthur and I were shocked and surprised. Lucy's face was almost angry. She closed her mouth and her eyes and went back to sleep. Her breathing was weak again.

'Now you can kiss her,' said the professor.

Arthur held her hand and kissed her. A few moments later, she died.

Arthur is a broken man. We all three loved her, but Arthur was hers. It's terrible to see him. It was strange, but when she died, some of her colour came back to her. Usually people are paler when they die. But Lucy almost looked better. I turned to the professor. 'She's beautiful, isn't she? She's so peaceful. It's difficult to believe that she's dead. Now she can have some peace. It's all over[1] for her.'

'Yes, she is beautiful, but this is not the end. It is only the beginning. Wait and see,' he said.

We made the preparations for Lucy's funeral. The professor put some garlic flowers in her coffin. He put a gold cross on her mouth.

Mina Harker's Diary – 24th September

Jonathan and I are now at home, in our new house. Today has been a terrible day. When we arrived home, there was a telegram for me. Lucy is dead. So is her mother. Their funeral was yesterday. She was my best friend.

Jonathan is asleep. He's still ill. He had a bad shock today. We were walking in London. Suddenly, Jonathan stopped. He looked very frightened. 'It's him! It's him!' he said.

He was looking at a tall, thin man. The man was very pale and had long, white teeth. He had a very hard face. I didn't like him. Jonathan took my arm and we ran away. When we got home, he gave me his diary. He has asked me to read it.

---

1. **all over:** 一切都過去了

From The Westminster Gazette – 27th September

A HAMPSTEAD MYSTERY

Strange things are happening in Hampstead. Last night, the police found a small child in the park. It was very late at night. The boy was very weak. He had two small marks on his neck. The marks are something like marks that an animal could make. Like a bite[1] from a dog. The police took him to hospital. When he was feeling a little better, the boy talked about the *Bloofer Lady*.

This is not the first time. A similar thing happened two nights ago. Three other children also came home with marks on their necks. They all talked about the *Bloofer Lady*. Police think the children mean the *Beautiful Lady*.

The police are watching for small children alone, late at night. They are also looking out for a dog.

Letter from Professor Van Helsing to Mina Harker – 28th September

Dear Mrs Harker,

My name is Professor Van Helsing. I am a friend of Dr Seward and Arthur Holmwood.

I am writing to you, because I helped poor Lucy before she died. Arthur gave me Lucy's letters and diary. I read them and I know you are her best friend. I think you can help me. I must speak to you soon.

Best wishes,

Van Helsing

Mina Harker's Diary – 30th September

I sent a telegram to Professor Van Helsing. He came to see me yesterday. He's a very nice man and he's very interesting. I gave Jonathan's diary to him. It's going to be very useful to him. I told him

---

1. **bite:** 咬傷痕跡

about the strange man Jonathan saw on Thursday. The professor is very worried about it. He's going to read Jonathan's diary. Then he's going to talk to me again.

Jonathan Harker's diary – 2nd October

This morning, I met Professor Van Helsing. He's a very kind and intelligent man. He's read my diary and some of poor Lucy's letters. He wants to help me. He also wants me to help him.

Dr Seward's diary – 2nd October

This afternoon, the professor came to see me. He showed me a story in the newspaper. Someone, or something, is attacking children in Hampstead. The children have strange marks on their necks – the marks are exactly like the marks poor Lucy had.

The professor talked to me very seriously. He asked me to believe him and to trust him. I was shocked by what he said. He says the marks the children have on their necks weren't made by an animal. They were made by Lucy!

I don't see how this is possible. Lucy is dead. But the professor is certain. It seems mad to me, but I know the professor. He isn't mad.

Tonight, we're going to visit one of the children in hospital. Then we're going to the graveyard. We're going to watch. The professor says that we'll see Lucy.

Later

It's late, but I can't sleep. Tonight was an incredible night. I'm very shocked. We went to see the child in hospital. The marks on his neck are the same as the marks on Lucy's neck. The little boy talked about the *Bloofer Lady*. He wanted to go and play with her. The professor told the doctors and nurses to watch the child carefully.

After dinner, we went to the graveyard. It was quite late. The professor took a key from his pocket. He unlocked the Westenra tomb[1] and we went inside. In the light from his lamp, we read the names on the coffins. He found Lucy's coffin and started to open it. I was very shocked and I tried to stop him. But he continued. 'You must believe me. You must trust me!' he said. 'Now, look! Look inside!'

The coffin was empty. Lucy wasn't there. It was incredible.

The professor is coming again tomorrow. This time we're going to the tomb in the daytime. He says I need to see something more.

3ʳᵈ October

We went to the Westenra tomb this morning. The professor opened Lucy's coffin again. This time she was inside it. I was very surprised. The professor explained to me that she isn't dead. She isn't alive. Poor, poor Lucy. She is Un-dead. The marks on her neck came from a vampire. Now, she's a vampire too. Her teeth are very long; like a dog's teeth. The professor says that Lucy is the *Bloofer Lady*. She's biting the children. Lucy is drinking their blood. It's horrible!

He says we must save her and we must save the children. He says we must kill her. If we kill her, then she'll be safe. He wants Arthur to help us, too. I don't know what to think. How can we kill Lucy? She's already dead. But it's true. She isn't the lovely Lucy any more. She's a vampire and a monster. I hope Arthur will understand, too.

Later

This afternoon, Arthur, Quincey and I all went to meet the professor. He told Arthur and Quincey that we must go to Lucy's

---

1. **tomb:** 墳墓

tomb. He said that we must open her coffin. Arthur was very angry, but listened to the professor's story. I also told Arthur about Lucy's empty coffin yesterday. Then I told him about this morning. The professor explained to Arthur that Lucy is Un-dead[1]. The only way to save Lucy, is to kill her. He said we must put garlic in her mouth. We must cut off[2] her head and put a stake[3] through her heart. Arthur thought this was horrible. He said the professor mustn't do it. The professor asked Arthur to trust him.

After dinner, we all went to the graveyard. We opened Lucy's coffin. Arthur and Quincy were very scared. Then they looked inside; it was empty. They were very shocked. The professor closed the coffin and we all went outside. The professor locked the door of the tomb. He put garlic around the door. He put a cross on the outside of the door. Then, we all waited behind some trees.

After a short time, we saw a woman in the graveyard. She was holding something. Then we heard a small cry; it was a child's cry. The woman came nearer and we could see her in the moonlight. It was Lucy! But she wasn't the same lovely Lucy. Her face was hard and evil. She looked horrible. Arthur was very shocked. We went towards her. She was standing by the door of the tomb. The professor held up his lamp. She was holding a small child. There, on Lucy's face, we could see blood. There was blood all around her mouth. There was blood on her dress. Her eyes were red and angry. She saw us and threw the child onto the earth. Then she saw Arthur. She came towards him and opened her arms to him. Arthur wanted to kiss her. Luckily, the professor stopped him. The professor stood in front of Lucy with a cross in his hand. She didn't like it and ran back towards

1. Un-dead: 不死人
2. cut off: 切掉

3. stake: 椿

the tomb. She was very angry. Her face was horrible. Arthur began to understand. Then the professor took away the garlic and the cross on the door. Lucy went inside. She went inside through a small gap, without opening the door. Now we're *all* sure; Lucy is Un-dead.

We took the poor child to the hospital. I hope he'll live. The professor says we must go back to the graveyard in the daytime. We must kill Lucy, tomorrow.

Stop & Check

1 **Are the statements True (T) or False (F)? Correct the false statements.**

	T	F
1 When Lucy dies, the marks on her neck disappear.	☐	☐
2 The professor puts some onion flowers in Lucy's coffin.	☐	☐
3 Jonathan sees a strange man in London.	☐	☐
4 Police think *Bloofer Lady* means *Blue Lady*.	☐	☐
5 Professor Van Helsing visits Mina and Jonathan Harker.	☐	☐
6 Dr Seward and the professor visit a child at his house.	☐	☐
7 They decide not to open Lucy's coffin.	☐	☐
8 Lucy's teeth are like cat's teeth.	☐	☐
9 The professor tells Arthur and Quincey about Lucy.	☐	☐
10 They think Lucy looks lovely.	☐	☐

Grammar

2 **Present Perfect v. Past Simple. Read the newspaper article. Cross out the incorrect form of the verb.**

Missing Children

Three young children disappeared/have disappeared from their homes near Hampstead. Their parents (**1**) spoke/have spoken to the police last night when they (**2**) didn't come/haven't come home for supper. "We (**3**) looked/have looked everywhere, but our search is continuing," said a policeman. "We are very worried about the children. We (**4**) <u>asked/</u> <u>have asked</u> parents to watch their children carefully."

This is not the first case of missing children. Two days ago, a boy (**5**) <u>didn't come/hasn't come</u> home until very late. When he (**6**) <u>arrived/</u> <u>has arrived</u> home, he (**7**) <u>had/has had</u> two small marks on his neck. More details in tomorrow's Gazette.

Writing for KEY

3 **Imagine you are Mina. Read part of the note from Professor Van Helsing again.**

> *I know you are her best friend. Now I think you can help me. Can I speak to you soon?*
>
> *Best wishes*
>
> *Van Helsing*

Write a note to the professor.
Write 25-35 words.
Say:
- what day you want to meet him.
- what time you want to meet him.
- where you want to meet him.

PRE-READING ACTIVITY

Speaking

4a **We learn more about Renfield and his animals in Chapter Seven. Put these animals in order. Number 1 is your least favourite and number 9 is your favourite.**

☐ fly   ☐ snake   ☐ bat
☐ mosquito   ☐ rat   ☐ cat
☐ mouse   ☐ spider   ☐ dog

4b **Compare your answers in pairs. Say why you like them/don't like them.**

Finding the Boxes

▶ 11 *Dr Seward's Diary (continued) – 4th October*

Arthur, Quincey, the professor and I all went to the graveyard together. The professor unlocked the door of the tomb. He had a large bag with him. We went over to Lucy's coffin and the professor opened it. Inside, Lucy still had blood around her mouth. She looked hard and horrible. Arthur looked at her. His face was hard, too. He now hated her. This *thing* wasn't Lucy. This *thing* was a vampire.

'Now, Arthur. You loved her more than any of us,' said the professor. 'You have the right to save her. Do you want to help her?'

'Yes, tell me what I must do,' said Arthur, bravely.

'Use this hammer[1]; use it to hammer this stake through her heart. We must all pray[2].'

Arthur took the stake and hammered it into the vampire's heart. The monster screamed. It was a horrible scream. A river of blood came out of its mouth. The body shook and shook. Then more blood came out of its heart. Blood was everywhere. But Arthur didn't stop. He hammered and hammered. We prayed and prayed. After a while, the vampire stopped shaking. There was silence. We all looked at the

1. **hammer:** 錘子
2. **pray:** 祈禱

vampire in the coffin. It was Lucy. She looked beautiful. She wasn't a monster any more. Arthur kissed her. 'Now you're free!' he said.

Arthur and Quincey went outside. The professor and I cut off the top of the stake. We left the rest of it in Lucy's heart. Then, we cut off her head. We filled her mouth with garlic. The professor closed the coffin and we went outside too. The professor locked the door of the tomb. 'Now, my friends,' he said, 'we have finished the first part of our work. The next part is to find Count Dracula. We must destroy[1] him. I must go back to Holland. I need some more information. Now, let's go back to my hotel. We must make a plan. I want you to meet Mina and Jonathan Harker. They are coming to Carfax to stay with you, Seward. We must all work together.'

The professor gave me a copy of Jonathan's diary. The professor says it will help me understand everything.

5th October

Earlier today, I went to meet Mina Harker at the station. I recognised her immediately from Lucy's description of her. She shook my hand warmly. The professor is right: she's a very good, intelligent lady. Her husband, Jonathan, is coming later. He's gone to Whitby to find out more about the fifty boxes of earth.

Later, I showed Mina my phonograph. She thinks it's a wonderful machine. She thinks it's even better than using shorthand. In some ways, I agree with her. But there's a problem. If I want to listen to my diary, sometimes it's difficult to find the right part, or the right day. Mina's going to help me. She has brought her typewriter with her. She's going to type my diary for me. I think that's a good idea. It'll be difficult for her to read, but I want her to know all about Lucy. I've

1. **destroy:** 消滅

read Jonathan's diary. Mina wants me to read her diary, too. We all think the time has come to share. We need to destroy Count Dracula. There must be no secrets between us.

I hope that Jonathan will find out a lot in Whitby. We need to know about the boxes. Where did they go? If we find out about them, we can find the count. We can destroy him.

Jonathan Harker's diary – 7th October

I met Mr Billington at the station in Whitby and he immediately took me to his offices. He's a friend of my employer, Mr Hawkins. He was very happy to help me. He gave me a lot of information about the boxes: the fifty boxes which the count sent here to England. The letter with them said '50 boxes of earth, for scientific research'. Mr Billington sent the boxes to London, on the instructions[1] of the count. He sent them to Kings Cross Station.

When I got back to London, I went to speak to the officers at the station. Fifty boxes of earth arrived and two men took all fifty of them to a chapel. Where's the chapel? Near Dr Seward's hospital, in Carfax!

I'm now sure that all the boxes of earth arrived in Carfax. But are they all still there? I don't know. We must find out as soon as possible.

Dr Seward's diary – 7th October

Jonathan returned from Whitby today. He's a very nice man. The professor's also arriving today. And Arthur and Quincey are arriving later today, too. Mina has finished typing up my diary. Jonathan and Mina are putting together all the information from all our diaries and

---

1. **instructions:** 指示

letters. They want to put everything in order of time and date. It's going to be very interesting. Jonathan has also brought some of the letters from Mr Hawkins, his employer. They're about the count's house. And some of them are from the count's lawyer, Mr Billington. There's information in them about the count's instructions and his movements. There's also information about the boxes. The dates are very interesting. They seem to have a link with Renfield. There's a link with Renfield's violence and the dates: the dates of the count's movements. I'm sure there's a connection between Renfield and the count. The letters are going to help us.

This afternoon, I went to visit Renfield in his room. He's very quiet. In fact, he doesn't seem mad at all. He saw Mina in the gardens this afternoon. He asked me about her. 'Who's that woman? She isn't the woman you wanted to marry. That woman's dead. I know she is.'

I was surprised. How did Renfield know about Lucy?

Later

After dinner, we all met in my study. It was good to see the professor again. The professor put his golden cross on the table. We all held hands. We made a promise together. We promised to find the count. We promised to destroy him.

The professor's plan is very good. First, we must go to the great house and search the chapel. We must find the boxes and we must sterilise[1] them. The professor wants Mina to stay here. She'll be safe here. We're going to the big house later tonight.

While we were talking, Quincey jumped out of his chair. He pointed at the window. There was a huge bat there. It was trying to get inside.

---

1. **sterilise:** 給……消毒

Jonathan Harker's diary – 8th October 4 a.m.

We've just returned from Carfax. I can't sleep, so I'm writing this. The professor gave each of us a cross and some garlic. He took out some skeleton keys[1] from his pocket. I tried some of them. One of them worked perfectly. I unlocked the door and we went inside the house. There was a horrible smell: a smell of death and dying. We went from room to room. There were boxes and papers and letters everywhere. In one room, hundreds of rats appeared. It was horrible. We only found 29 boxes. 21 boxes are missing! We must find the other boxes!

While I'm writing, I'm looking at my lovely Mina. She's asleep and she's so beautiful. Perhaps she's a little pale. I hope she isn't ill. I'll ask her in the morning.

Mina Harker's diary – 8th October

I woke up very late this morning. In the night, I had a strange dream. I don't want to tell Jonathan. I don't want him to worry. In my dream, I heard a lot of dogs howling. There was a large bat. Then it wasn't a bat, it was Renfield. Then it wasn't Renfield. There was a person with very red eyes. There was a white fog. Then I saw a very white face, very close to mine. Then everything became black and dark. I didn't like it. Today, I feel very tired. I'm worried about this dream. It's like one of the dreams in Jonathan's diary. I think I'll ask Dr Seward for some medicine tonight. Perhaps he's got some medicine to help me sleep.

---

1. skeleton keys: 百合匙，又稱萬能鑰匙

Jonathan Harker's diary – 8th October, evening

This afternoon, I spoke to some of the workmen in the village. I asked them about the boxes. Two of the men delivered the boxes to London. They delivered[1] 6 to an address in south London and 6 to an address in the north. They say I need to speak to a man called Sam Bloxam. He probably knows about the other boxes. I'm going to London tomorrow. I think Count Dracula is making homes for himself all over London. We must stop him.

9th October

What an exciting day! I've found all the boxes! Mr Bloxam was very helpful. He delivered the boxes to different addresses. At each address, there was a tall, thin man there. The man helped Mr Bloxam with the boxes. The man was very pale and very, very strong; he had strange red eyes. Mr Bloxam saw the count! Count Dracula is definitely in London!

I'm still worried about Mina. She looks very pale and tired.

Dr Seward's diary – 9th October

Renfield's changing from one moment to the next. One minute he's happy and calm. Then the next, he's violent, angry or depressed. Some of the nurses say they can hear him in his room at night. Sometimes he's talking very loudly. They think he's talking to himself, or that he's praying.

Earlier today, he was very calm, but depressed. He talked about life. He talked about the life of the flies, the spiders, the birds and all the animals he has eaten. He's afraid of their ghosts. I'm now certain that he has a link with the count. When I left, he seemed confused.

---

1. delivered: 運送

Later, I heard him singing in his room. He seemed very happy.

10th October

How can I start? This has been an incredible day. Late last night, I went to see Renfield. He was lying on the floor. There was blood all over him: he was badly hurt. I cleaned the blood and put Renfield into bed. He was thirsty, so I gave him some water. He talked about the count. I asked a nurse to find the professor, Quincey and Arthur. Renfield told us his story; we all listened very carefully.

The count has often been inside the hospital. He has visited Renfield and has given him flies, spiders and sometimes rats. The count can get into buildings through very small gaps. Then, the incredible news. The count has recently visited Mina!

But where was the count now? There was no time to lose. We ran to Mina's room. Jonathan was on the bed and his eyes were closed. He couldn't move. Count Dracula was there! There was a cut on the count's chest. The count had his hands on Mina's neck. He was holding her very tightly.[1] She was drinking the count's blood. The count was making her do it. It was horrible! He looked up. His eyes were red and his face was incredibly pale. He threw Mina onto the floor and came towards us. The professor stood in front of him with the cross and the garlic. We were ready to kill him. Then the moon went behind a cloud. The room went dark and the count escaped out of the window.

We gave Jonathan some water and he woke up. He saw the blood and he saw Mina. He held her. She was very, very frightened. She cried and cried, 'I'm unclean. I'm unclean,' she repeated over and over again[2].

I went back to look after Renfield. But there was nothing more I could do for him. Later that night, the poor man died.

1. **tightly:** 緊緊
2. **over and over again:** 再三

Stop & Check

1 **Choose the best answer - A, B, or C.**

1 Why did the Professor go back to Holland?

A ☐ He needed to see a friend.
B ☐ He needed to buy some garlic flowers.
C ☐ He needed to find some more information.

2 Who did Dr Seward meet at the station?

A ☐ Arthur Holmwood.
B ☐ Mina Harker.
C ☐ Renfield.

3 How did Mina help Dr Seward?

A ☐ She typed his diary.
B ☐ She typed his letter.
C ☐ She typed his story.

4 Where did Mr Billington send the boxes?

A ☐ He sent them to Whitby.
B ☐ He sent them to the abbey.
C ☐ He sent them to London.

5 What did the friends do after dinner?

A ☐ They held hands and made a promise.
B ☐ They ate garlic.
C ☐ They read the newspaper.

6 What did Quincey see at the window?

A ☐ A large bird.
B ☐ A large bat.
C ☐ A black cloud.

7 Who did the friends find in Mina's room?

A ☐ Renfield.
B ☐ Sam Bloxam.
C ☐ Count Dracula.

2 Look at Mina Harker's typing. Find the mistakes and correct them. There are two mistakes in each statement.

1 Jonathan has <u>brouhgt</u> some of the letters from his empolyer.

_____*brought*_____   _____

2 They're about the count's hause. Some of them are from the count's lavyer.

_____   _____

3 There's infromation in them about the count's instrucsions.

_____   _____

4 The dates are very intresting. They seem to hav a link with Renfield.

_____   _____

5 The dates link Renfield's violance with the count's moovements.

_____   _____

6 I'm sure their's a conection between Renfield and the count.

_____   _____

PRE-READING ACTIVITY

Vocabulary

3a In Chapter Eight, the characters travel a long way. Put the words in the box into the correct column. Then add a word of your own to each column.

train • plane • canoe • boat • car • bike • horse • coach

travel by road/rail	travel by sea	travel by air

3b Decide which means of transport is
  A the fastest **B** the slowest **C** the most comfortable **D** the safest **E** the most interesting.

Chapter Eight

Waiting for Count Dracula

12 *Dr Seward's diary (continued) – 11th October*

Mina and Jonathan talked to all of us today. Mina doesn't want to hurt anyone. She wants us to kill her, if she becomes dangerous. The professor knows this is wrong. If Mina dies now, she'll be Un-dead. We know from Lucy that the Un-dead are very dangerous. We must make sure Mina stays alive. That's the only way to save her and to save other people.

After lunch, we're going to the chapel in the big house. We're going to destroy the boxes there. We must do this during the day. We'll all be safe until the sun goes down.

Later

Before we went to the big house, the professor touched each person's head with a cross and prayed. When he touched Mina's head, she screamed. The cross made a mark on her head. Then, like last night, again she said, 'I'm unclean. I'm unclean.' She was in terrible pain[1].

We put her to bed and told her to rest for the afternoon. She agreed. Then we went to the big house. We all had our garlic and our crosses. We used the skeleton keys again. One by one, we opened the boxes. We put some garlic into each box and we made the sign

1. **in terrible pain:** 非常痛苦

of a cross in the earth. Then we closed the boxes again. We did this over and over again. Now the boxes are sterile. They're useless to the count. The great house, here in Carfax, is now safe. Tomorrow, we're going to London. We're going to visit all of Count Dracula's new houses. We're going to do the same thing with all the other boxes. We're going to destroy him and his houses.

12th October

Mina said goodbye to us and we went to the station. She's better today, but there's still a mark on her head. The professor had his skeleton keys. We went to the first house in London. The professor unlocked the door and we went inside. The smell was horrible. It smelled of death and dying. We looked around[1] the house. We found eight boxes. One box was missing! We also found a lot of keys: the keys to the other houses. In one room, we found letters with addresses: the addresses for the count's other houses. Quincey and Arthur went away with the keys. They went to sterilise the boxes in the other houses. The professor, Arthur and I stayed in the first house. We waited for Count Dracula. We waited to surprise him. We waited to kill him.

It seemed like a long time. Then we heard a sound at the door. All three of us held our crosses and our garlic. We were ready to attack. The door opened, but it was Quincey and Arthur. They were very pleased. All the boxes are now safely full of garlic. Each box has the sign of a cross in it. The boxes are sterile! We're winning!

All five of us now waited in the dark. We waited for the count. Finally, there was a noise at the door. It was the count. He ran into the room. His eyes were red and angry. He came towards us, ready to

---

1. **looked around:** 四處看看

attack. But we were all ready, too. We ran towards him with our garlic and our crosses. He shouted at us, 'I'm going to kill you all!'

Then, for a moment, he looked frightened. He saw the crosses and he ran to the window. He jumped out and ran away.

We went back to the station and came back here to Carfax. We didn't want to leave Mina alone after dark. Our work in London is done. But, where has the count gone now? We need to talk to Mina. The count often visited her in the hospital. Mina is the key. In some way, her head is linked with the count's head, in the same way that Renfield had links with the count. The professor says Mina will help us find the count. The professor wants to hypnotise[1] her. He says he can find out a lot about the count from her. I think it's a good idea. Mina thinks it's a good idea, too. She knows she can tell us a lot. With the count away from the great house, Mina's looking better.

13th October

Now we know! The professor hypnotised Mina today. In her sleep, she told us about the count. Like Renfield, in part, Mina is under the count's control. Count Dracula has a plan to escape. He's going to escape on a ship. He's going to go to Varna, a city on the Black Sea. Then he's going to go back to his castle. Perhaps we can stop him before his ship leaves. We must destroy him!

Jonathan and I went to the port. Unfortunately, a ship left for Varna this afternoon. We asked the port officer about the passengers. There weren't very many people on the ship. Jonathan described the count. Yes, the count was one of the passengers.

We went back to the hospital in Carfax. We made a plan. We're going to follow the count. We're going to travel on land as much as

1. **hypnotise:** 催眠

possible. Travelling on land is quicker than travelling by ship. We can get to Varna before the count's ship. We can wait for him at the port in Varna. Then, we can attack him and kill him.

14ᵗʰ October

Mina's changing. We're all worried about her. Just like Renfield, in the daytime, she's free and happy. At night, she's pale and weak. We must be careful to watch her. We mustn't leave her alone[1]. But Mina is a very brave lady. She knows she's changing. She wants us to be safe. She thinks she's communicating with Dracula in her sleep. She thinks she can help us.

★ ★ ★

Dr Seward's diary (continued) – 4ᵗʰ January

We have done it. Count Dracula is dead! We have destroyed him.

It was a long journey to Varna. We waited there for a week. The ship didn't arrive. We asked at the port office. At first, no-one had any news for us. Then we heard that the count's ship was in Galatz. He wasn't coming to Varna. We couldn't believe it. How did he know we were in Varna? Was it Mina? Was she still communicating with him? The professor hypnotised her again. She gave us some important information. The count was going home. She could see him; he was travelling by boat.

Quickly, we made a plan. We decided to go to the castle in 3 pairs. Arthur and Jonathan went by boat on the River Danube. Quincey and I went on horses. Mina and the professor went by train and then by coach.

Mina and the professor reached the castle first. It was snowing and it was very cold. It was getting dark and the count wasn't there. They

---

1. **leave her alone:** 留下她一個人

made beds for themselves in the dining room. The professor made a circle of earth around Mina's bed. He touched it with his cross. Then he put garlic all around the circle. That night, three women visited Mina and the professor. The women tried to get into the dining room. They wanted Mina to go with them. They wanted to drink the professor's blood.

The following day, the professor went to the chapel. He destroyed the three women. He sterilised the count's box with the cross and the garlic. Then, Quincey and I arrived. Mina and the professor were still waiting for the count. Then, in the distance, we saw his coach: the huge black horses and the strange blue lights. There were two men on horses behind him. They were Arthur and Jonathan!

The count arrived at the castle and went to the chapel. We all ran into the chapel behind him. He screamed when he saw his box. He turned towards us, his red eyes full of hate. Quincey ran towards him, but the count was too fast. The count killed Quincey. Jonathan quickly attacked the count and cut his throat. He hammered a stake through the count's heart. The screaming was terrible. Then, strangely, the count's face was calm. He smiled for a moment. Count Dracula was dead.

★ ★ ★

All the events of the last 6 months seem like a distant memory[1]. Mina is well again, so is Jonathan. The professor is back in Holland. And Arthur is learning to live life without dear Lucy.

In the spring, we're all going to meet again. It'll be sad to be together, without Quincey. But it'll be good to see everyone else again. ▣

1. a distant memory: 遙遠的回憶

Stop & Check

1 **Fill the gaps in the text.**

Mina (**1**) _said_ goodbye to us and we went (**2**) _____ the station. She's better today, but there's still a mark on her head. The professor had his skeleton (**3**) _____. We went to the first house in London. The professor unlocked the (**4**) _____ and we went inside. The smell was horrible. It smelled of death and dying. We looked around the house. We found eight boxes. One box (**5**) _____ missing! We also found a (**6**) _____ of keys: the keys to the other houses. In one room, we found letters (**7**) _____ addresses: the addresses for the count's other houses. Quincey and Arthur went away with (**8**) _____ keys.

Vocabulary

2a **Find the odd one out in each group. Write why. Your answer can be different from other people's answers.**

1 **A** ☐ garlic **B** ☐ onion **C** ☐ carrot **D** ☐ lemon

_____

2 **A** ☐ December **B** ☐ Winter **C** ☐ July **D** ☐ February

_____

3 **A** ☐ house **B** ☐ caravan **C** ☐ flat **D** ☐ office

_____

4 **A** ☐ London **B** ☐ Tokyo **C** ☐ Toronto **D** ☐ Paris

_____

2b **Design your own odd one out activity for your partner.**

Reading for KEY

3 **Which notice (A-G) says this (1-5).**

1 You don't have to pay, if you're older than sixty.

2 If you find someone, you will get some money.

3 You can visit people at 6pm on Wednesdays.

4 You can save money here, if you are travelling.

5 You can eat here, even if you aren't staying.

A

Special Train Fares
30% off
This weekend only

B

BUDAPEST ART GALLERY
Over-60s free

C

REWARD
Count Dracula
If you have any information
call the police on 999

D

<u>MISSING!</u>
Three small children
Last seen in Hampstead
call the police on 999

E

```
URGENT!
AM ARRIVING KING'S CROSS STATION.
WEDS. 6 PM
VAN H
```

F

Hospital
Visiting Hours
Noon-1pm & 6-8pm weekdays
All day Sunday

G

HOTEL ROYAL, KLAUSENBURGH
International Menu
Open to non-residents

Bram Stoker (1847 – 1912)

Bram Stoker.

Early Life

Bram Stoker's full name was Abraham Stoker and he had the same name as his father. He was born in Clontarf, a suburb of Dublin. He had six brothers and sisters. Bram Stoker was ill when he was a child, and spent most of his time in bed. His mother read to him. He had a lot of time to listen to stories and think. When he was seven years old, Bram got better and went to a local school. When he left school, Bram went to Trinity College, Dublin. He studied mathematics there and was a very clever student.

Bram Stoker and the Theatre

When he was a student, Bram Stoker became very interested in the theatre. He wrote about theatre and plays for a Dublin newspaper. In Dublin, he met Henry Irving – a very famous actor. Irving was the actor/manager of the Lyceum Theatre in London. In 1878, Bram Stoker married Florence Balcombe and they moved to London. Bram Stoker became the manager of the Lyceum Theatre and assistant to Henry Irving. He managed the Lyceum for many years.

Writing

Bram Stoker started writing when he lived in Dublin. As well as being a journalist, he wrote other works of non-fiction. When he moved to London, Bram Stoker began to write fiction, too. He knew many other writers, including Oscar Wilde, Arthur Conan Doyle and Walt Whitman. Bram Stoker published *Dracula* in 1897. It is his most famous novel, but he wrote other stories, too. He also continued to write non-fiction, including Henry Irving's biography. The biography was more successful than *Dracula* at the time.

The first edition of Dracula, 1897.

Later Years

Bram Stoker was quite well-known in literary London, but his books weren't very popular. He was a hard worker, but he didn't earn much money. He was often ill in his later years and he died in April 1912 at the age of sixty-four. He died in London. There is a memorial to Bram Stoker in Golders Green Cemetery.

Dracula's Success

When Bram Stoker published *Dracula* in 1897, not everyone liked it. Some critics said it was too real. They didn't think it was 'good art'. Other critics thought it was brilliant. The first film of *Dracula* was early in cinema history, in 1922. Many more films followed, including Francis Ford Coppola's 1992 version, *Bram Stoker's Dracula*. There are translations of *Dracula* in many languages. There is even a cartoon based on the character of Count Dracula; *Count Duckula*.

Task

Complete the form with the information about Bram Stoker.

Full Name: _____

Place of Birth: _____

Date of Birth: _____

Studied: _____

Name of Wife: _____

Job at the Lyceum Theatre: _____

Date of Death: _____

Communication & Technology in *Dracula*

Bram Stoker was interested in technology. He writes a lot about the new technologies of the time in *Dracula*. Of course, these technologies all had problems – just like technology today.

Shorthand.

Shorthand and Stenography

In *Dracula*, Mina and Jonathan both use shorthand. This is a special way of writing that uses symbols. It is a very fast system – much faster than writing by hand. This was really important in the days before computers. At the time Bram Stoker was writing, the most popular system of shorthand was Pitman. Sir Isaac Pitman invented the system in 1837. Shorthand is still used by journalists today. Stenography is another name for writing, or typing, in shorthand (see photo). What was the problem? You had to learn the symbols before you could write or read shorthand.

A stenographer.

Kodak

Film on a roll.

In *Dracula*, Jonathan uses his Kodak to take a photograph of the house to show Count Dracula. Photography developed very quickly in the nineteenth century. The first permanent photo was taken in 1826, but taking photographs was very expensive and difficult. This changed with Kodak technology at the time of Bram Stoker's work. Kodak was actually the first company to produce film on a roll (see photo). This made photography cheaper and easier for people. When you took a picture with Kodak, your picture went onto a light-sensitive film. What were the problems with this system? You couldn't take one picture then look at it straight away; you had to finish the film. If you opened the camera, light destroyed the film – and your pictures. You also had to pay a specialist to print out your pictures.

The Typewriter and QWERTY

In the late nineteenth century, one of the major new inventions was the typewriter. In *Dracula*, Mina Harker is a typist. The typewriter was very important for business: before its invention, people had to write everything by hand. One big problem with the typewriter was the keyboard. Because it was mechanical, the keys often hit each other. Then the typist had to stop and unblock the keys. This meant that typing was slow. Some very clever people designed the QWERTY keyboard to stop this from happening. Typists soon became very fast and the keys didn't hit each other very much. Have you got a QWERTY keyboard on the computer you use today? Take a look at the first six letters on your keyboard (start from the top left).

A typewriter.

The Phonograph

If you look at the illustration on page 33 of the book, you can see Dr Seward speaking into his phonograph. He is recording his diary. The technology for recording voices was very new at the time. Thomas Edison invented the phonograph in 1877. It was important, because it could record sound and play it back – other machines could only record. The phonograph recorded sound onto a cylinder (a type of tube). Dr Seward's problem with the technology was that he couldn't find information easily on his cylinder.

Task

Discuss these questions in pairs.

1 Imagine Bram Stoker is going to write *Dracula* next year. What technology will his characters use
- for writing notes?
- for writing long documents?
- for taking photographs?
- for recording voices?

2 Will there be any problems with these technologies?

BATS
Do you like bats? Some people do and some people don't. But, if you look at the science, bats are very interesting animals.

Types of Bat

There are more than a thousand different types of bats in the world. We find more species (types) every year. Flying foxes and fruit bats are the largest bat species and they can weigh about 1.5 kg. The smallest is called the bumble bee bat and it only weighs about 2 grams! Bats are **mammals**; they are the only mammals which can really fly.

mammal (n)   an animal which is born from its mother's body. It drinks milk from its mother.

Habitat

In towns and cities, bats usually live in roofs. The place where they live is called a **roost**. These roosts are not permanent; bats often like to have their families in a different place from where they **hibernate**. Other bat habitats include forests, mountains, the coast and deserts. You can't see bats in the Arctic or Antarctica.

roost (n + v)   a place where some birds and bats go to sleep.

hibernate (v)   to go to sleep during the winter.

Diet

Most bats are **carnivores**. Some bats eat insects. One bat can eat 3,000 insects in one night. The city of Milan, Italy puts special bat boxes in parks and gardens where bats can live. This is because bats eat so many insects. Larger bat species sometimes eat fruit. There are some species of bats which eat small birds and frogs. Vampire bats also exist, but they are very rare. They drink the blood of mammals or birds. Bats can fly for very long distances to find food.

carnivore (n)   an animal that eats meat.

Echolocation

Bats use sounds to find their way. They send sounds to the area around them and then they feel the vibration from this sound. This is called an *echo*. The technical name for this type of finding your way is echolocation. Because they are **nocturnal**, bats need echolocation to help them fly in the dark. Echolocation helps them make a map of their location, but it also helps them find insects to eat. Bats can see, but their eyes are usually small. They don't need to use their eyes much.

As well as echolocation, bats have a very good sense of smell and good hearing.

nocturnal (adj) nocturnal animals are active at night.

Bats in Danger

There are many dangers to bats and a lot of them come from humans. Often, we build on their natural habitats. Many bats can change habitats, but others can't. Sometimes, people are afraid of bats; people then kill them and take away their roosts. Some scientists think that modern technology like Wi-Fi and mobile phones may cause problems to bats. It is possible that these technologies cause problems with echolocation. Fortunately, a lot of people are working hard to help bats and their habitats, too.

Task - Vocabulary

Choose a word from the above and answer the questions.

1 diurnal (adj) - diurnal animals are active during the day.
_____ (antonym)

2 herbivore (n) - an animal that doesn't eat meat.
_____ (antonym)

3 nest (n + v) - a place where some birds and animals go to eat and sleep. _____ (synonym)

4 reptile (n) - a cold-blooded animal like a crocodile or a snake. Reptiles are born from eggs. _____ (antonym)

TEST YOURSELF 自測

How much can you remember about the story of *Dracula*? Use the clues to complete the crossword.

Clues Across

1 Mina t_____ Dr Seward's diary. (5 letters)

2 Lucy isn't strong, she's w_____ . (4 letters)

3 Mina is learning to write s_____ . (9 letters)

5 The professor puts g_____ flowers in Lucy's room. (6 letters)

7 Jonathan has a bad d_____ . (5 letters)

9 Jonathan never sees the count e_____ or drink. (3 letters)

10 Jonathan is a p_____ . (8 letters)

Clues Down

1 Count Dracula has t_____ like a dog. (5 letters)

3 Renfield likes flies and s_____ . (7 letters)

4 Lucy and Mina look at ships in the h_____ . (7 letters)

6 Count Dracula lives in a c_____ . (6 letters)

8 Lucy has strange m_____ on her neck. (5 letters)

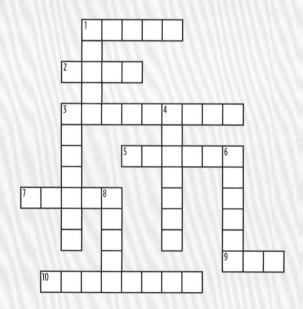

SYLLABUS 語法重點和學習主題

Nouns:
abstract nouns, compound nouns, noun phrases

Pronouns:
relative: *who*, *which*, *that*

Connectives:
and, *so*, *but*, *or*, *when*, *where*, *because*, *if*

Adjectives:
opinion, description, classification, participles as adjectives, predicative and attributive

Prepositions:
places, time, movement, phrases, *like*

Verbs:
TENSE, ASPECT, FORM:
Present Perfect Simple: indefinite past, recent past with *just*; Present Perfect v Past Simple; Past Continuous: continuous action interrupted by the Past Simple Tense; Future with *going to*; *-ing* form after verbs and prepositions; Present Simple Passive; *will* for future reference, promises & predictions; *need* for necessity & obligation; *could* for ability, requests and suggestions; *have to* for obligation; common phrasal verbs

Types of Clauses:
zero and type-one conditionals; defining relative clauses: *who*, *where*, zero pronoun

Answer Key 答案

Dracula

Pages 6-7

1 2 left
3 hid
4 saw
5 woke
6 threw
7 wrote
8 heard
9 flew
10 learnt
11 could

B	F	L	E	W	N	U	S
S	U	T	C	O	U	L	D
O	T	O	S	K	U	D	E
W	R	O	T	E	D	L	Y
D	D	K	A	H	I	D	S
I	L	H	E	A	R	D	S
L	E	A	R	N	T	E	A
R	F	T	K	V	E	E	W
R	T	A	R	M	E	R	R

2 1 e
2 d
3 b
4 c
5 f
6 a

3a Various answers

3b beautiful - ugly
dangerous - safe
dark - light
fat - thin
huge - small
modern - old

Pages 16-17

1 2A - 3C - 4B - 5A - 6A

2a 2 Is there a library?
3 Can Jonathan go into all the rooms?
4 Does Jonathan like his room?

5 What can Jonathan hear outside?
6 What does Count Dracula do with Jonathan's mirror?

3 2 forest (e)
3 field (a)
4 hill (f)
5 cliff (c)
6 river (d)

4a 2F - 3F - 4T - 5F - 6T - 7T - 8F

Pages 26-27

1 Dear Lucy,
How are you? I'm fine. I'm *studying* a lot at the moment. I'm learning to write in *shorthand*. I want to help Jonathan with his work. I'm also learning to use a *typewriter*. I'm now quite good. When Jonathan and I are married, I can type his work for him. I had a *letter* from him yesterday. He's coming back soon. He's writing a *diary*. I'm going to write a diary, too. A lot of people say it's very good for you. They say it helps your memory.
I'm really looking forward to seeing you. I've *never* been to Whitby. I love the sea and I love the sea air.
Tell me everything, when you write to me. I haven't had any news from you for a long time. I've heard some stories about a *tall*, handsome man! Who is he? Write soon,
Love Mina

2a face – teeth – neck – nose – head – lips – ears - eyes

2b sharp - teeth, nose
red - face, neck, nose, lips, ears, eyes
long - face, teeth, neck, nose, ears
white - face, teeth, neck, nose, lips, ears

3a 1 e - 2 a - 3 c - 4 b - 5 d

3b 1 interesting
2 silent
3 dangerous
4 light

4 **2C - 3B - 4B - 5C - 6C**

Pages 36-37

1 8 – 4 – 7 – 3 – 5 – 1 – 6 – 2

2a 2 has
3 go
4 some
5 in
6 lots
7 to
8 soon

3a

Q=A	W=B	E=C	R=D	T=E	Y=F	U=G	I=H
O=I	P=J	A=K	S=L	D=M	F=N	G=O	H=P
J=Q	K=R	L=S	Z=T	X=U	C=V	V=W	B=X
N=Y	M=Z						

THERE IS A STRANGE MAN ON MY SHIP. WE NEED HELP

3b **This code - XLTL ZIT ATNL OF ZIT GKRTK ZITN QKT GF Q ATNWGQKR**
This code - USES THE KEYS IN THE ORDER THEY ARE ON A KEYBOARD

Pages 46-47

1 2 Yes, he is.
3 Yes, she is.
4 Yes, she does.

5 No, they aren't.
6 Yes, he is.
7 Yes, he does.

2 You mustn't worry.
Can you pick me up...
I will arrive...
I won't be late.
I can help...
Can I stay...

3a POSSIBLE ANSWERS
How much does it cost?
Where will we stay?
When will we leave?
What can / shall / will we do? What are we going to do?
Is there a website?

4a 2 worse
3 bad
4 worse
5 paler and paler
6 red

Pages 56-57
1 2 G - 3 A - 4 C - 5 F - 6 H - 7 B - 8 D
2a 2 doctor
3 nurse
4 reporter
5 professor
6 lawyer
3 2A - 3A - 4A - 5C - 6A

Pages 66-67
1 1 T
2 F - He put some garlic flowers in her coffin.
3 T
4 F - They think it means *Beautiful Lady.*
5 T
6 F - They visit him in the hospital.
7 F - They open it.
8 F - They are like dog's teeth.
9 T
10 F - They think she looks horrible. Her face is hard and evil.
2 1 spoke
2 didn't come
3 have looked
4 have asked
5 didn't come
6 arrived
7 had

Pages 76-77
2 1C – 2B – 3A – 4C – 5A – 6B – 7 C
1 brought - employer
2 house - lawyer
3 information - instructions
4 interesting - have
5 violence - movements
6 there's - connection

3a **travel by road/rail**
   train
   car
   bike
   horse
   coach
   travel by sea
   canoe
   boat
   travel by air
   plane

Pages 84-85

1   (2)to
   (3)keys
   (4)door
   (5)was
   (6)lot
   (7)with
   (8)the

2a **1** Possible answers
   1 D The others are all vegetables.
   2 B The others are all months.
   3 B A caravan can move.
   4 C The others are all capital cities.

3   1B - 2C - 3F - 4A - 5G

Page 91

1   nocturnal
2   carnivore
3   roost
4   mammal

Page 92

Clues Across	Clues Down
1 types	1 teeth
2 weak	3 spiders
3 shorthand	4 harbour
5 garlic	6 castle
7 dream	8 marks
9 eat	
10 prisoner	

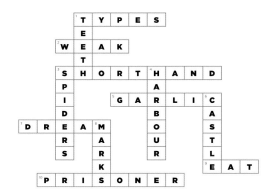

Read for Pleasure: *Dracula* 吸血殭屍

作　　者：Bram Stoker
改　　寫：Janet Borsbey and Ruth Swan
繪　　畫：Valerio Vidali
照　　片：Shutterstock
責任編輯：黃家麗
封面設計：涂慧　丁意
出　　版：商務印書館（香港）有限公司
　　　　　香港筲箕灣耀興道 3 號東滙廣場 8 樓
　　　　　http://www.commercialpress.com.hk
發　　行：香港聯合書刊物流有限公司
　　　　　香港新界大埔汀麗路 36 號中華商務印刷大廈 3 字樓
印　　刷：中華商務彩色印刷有限公司
　　　　　香港新界大埔汀麗路 36 號中華商務印刷大廈 14 字樓
版　　次：2017 年 3 月第 1 版第 1 次印刷
　　　　　© 2017 商務印書館（香港）有限公司
　　　　　ISBN 978 962 07 0475 8
　　　　　Printed in Hong Kong
　　　　　版權所有　不得翻印